the EVERAFTER

the EVERAFTER

amy huntley

Balzer + Bray

An Imprint of HarperCollins*Publishers*

Balzer + Bray is an imprint of HarperCollins Publishers.

The Everafter
Copyright © 2009 by Amy Huntley

Library of Congress Cataloging-in-Publication Data
Huntley, Amy.
    The everafter / Amy Huntley.—1st ed.
        p.   cm.
    Summary: After her death, seventeen-year-old Maddy finds a way to revisit
moments in her life by using objects that she lost while she was alive, and by so
doing she tries to figure out the complicated emotions, events, and meaning of her
existence.
    ISBN 978-0-06-177679-3 (trade bdg.) — ISBN 978-0-06-177680-9 (lib. bdg.)
    [1. Death—Fiction.   2. Dead—Fiction.   3. Friendship—Fiction.   4. Inter-
personal relations—Fiction.   5. Schools—Fiction.]   I. Title.
PZ7.H943Af   2009   2008046149
[Fic]—dc22   CIP
                                                                      AC

Typography by Carla Weise
09   10   11   12   13   LP/RRDB   10   9   8   7   6   5   4   3   2   1
❖
First Edition

There is a solitude of space
A solitude of sea
A solitude of death, but these
Society shall be
Compared with that profounder site
That polar privacy
A soul admitted to itself—
Finite infinity.
—EMILY DICKINSON

is

I'M DEAD.

Not my-parents-told-me-to-be-home-by-twelve-and-it's-two-o'clock-now dead. Just dead. Literally.

I think.

I can't feel a body anymore. No hunger—not even a stomach. No fingers to wiggle, no feet to tap.

So I pretty much have to assume that I'm . . . gone?

No. I can't be gone because I'm here.

I won't say that I've "passed on" or "passed away." I don't remember passing anything on the way here. For that matter, I don't remember dying, either. There's some saying about people "dying of curiosity." But I'm just curious about how I died.

Curious and . . . frightened. This place—wherever it is—surrounds me with vibrations. It just . . . *Is*.

Loneliness and mystery hum through me. I feel like I just woke up in a dark room that has no clock. And even worse: no people. Where is everyone I knew when I was alive? Who are they, and do they miss me? What if I'm in hell? Maybe instead of fire and brimstone, hell is just the feeling of loneliness. I don't remember much about being alive. I don't even remember my name. But loneliness being hell? That much I remember.

Ahead I see a bright pinprick of light. It seems my only chance for company. The prospect of reaching that light has replaced the throbbing ache of loneliness with a quivering hope.

I attempt to move toward the light, but the space that is . . . *Is* . . . cloaks me in thick, clinging darkness. It sticks to me like a disgustingly damp pair of jeans two sizes too small. I fight it out with *Is*, pushing against its boundaries, discovering I can get the bubble around me to expand if I try hard enough. But just as my space begins to grow, a cloud of loneliness surrounds me. I discover there's a reason the dead are stuffed into cozy coffins and small urns. This large empty space I've created makes me feel even more isolated.

I stop pushing against the boundaries of *Is*, and it shrinks into a small bubble again. All the energy that is me beats comfortably against the boundaries. Now that I am dead, I guess I have a soulbeat instead of a heartbeat.

Maybe some time passes. Maybe it doesn't. Hard to tell in this place. But one way or the other, I discover the problem with small, safe places.

They're boring.

I can't decide if my curiosity or my fear is the stronger emotion. And I don't quite understand how I can be feeling both if I'm dead. They chase each other around, circulating and percolating in me. Haunting me.

How is that possible? I mean, if I'm the one who's dead, how can something be haunting me? I'm supposed to be the one doing the haunting.

Finally, curiosity chases fear to the perimeter. It's time to explore.

Not that there's much to investigate. Just that bright pinprick of light.

I push against *Is* and expand the bubble of my space again. This time I discover I can intensify my soulbeat until it fills the bubble's space with energy. I ride the pulse of my soulbeat into the ever-expanding bubble as I approach the light.

It is a ring glowing in the dark. It shines against the midnight black of space like an X-ray. An image of a bracelet. What is it doing here?

As I get closer to the bracelet, I find myself floating right through the glowing circle of light. Photons scatter everywhere. I feel less lonely somehow with all this light swirling around me.

And because I can see now that there are more pinpricks of light.

They are little stars amid my dark existence, scattered across space at great distances. A spoon. A pair of socks, hair clips, pieces of paper, peas, a cell phone, keys, flowers, a handbag, a doll's shoe. More and more. They are artifacts of a life.

Mine?

I don't know why, but they seem to link me to all the people I sense I should be with.

I find still more: beads, photographs, a ring, a baby's rattle, and—how odd—a pair of underwear.

All these images are company at last.

But I need them to be closer together so I can spend time with all of them at once. Is there a way to click and drag them onto a desktop-sized space?

No. Apparently *Is* hasn't picked up on the whole wireless concept yet, and I will have to go to the ends of the Universe to find all my companions. I'd better start now if—

My trip has already come to an abrupt halt. I've hit the next object. It's a sweatshirt, and I can't bear the idea of moving on and leaving it behind.

I know it should make me feel warm, but its stark white glow fills me with longing. A sense of missing something— more intense than any feeling I've yet had—pounds through me. And suddenly I know I wasn't meant to be here alone. I know I expected to find Gabriel waiting for me.

But who is Gabriel?

the sweatshirt

I'M NOT SURE WHY this sweatshirt fascinates me so much. Maybe it's the missing smell. I sense that the most important thing about this sweatshirt is supposed to be its scent, but there aren't any smells in *Is*. I want to put the sweatshirt on, but I've got no body here in *Is*, either.

I try to remember what it felt like to have a body, and I imagine myself pulling warm fabric over my head. . . .

And then suddenly everything changes. Knowledge—not just some strange half memory—rips through me, scattering me across space and darkness, through nothingness and shadow. I am propelled toward harsh light. The sound of voices swells as I come closer and closer to them.

Metal chairs scrape across linoleum, adding an unharmonious musical accompaniment to the voices. Flickering specks of me hover, dancing in the air, and then unite into something not quite solid yet more substantial than I have been. I have a misty almost-form.

I'm back in the world.

In a classroom. An art classroom. I recognize myself, standing at a sink a few feet away. I'm trying to get red paint off my hands. I remember this moment—junior year, second-hour art class. A sense of joy at being back in the real world courses like blood through my almost-being, but it's strangely mixed with anger: I know that I'm about to discover that the sweatshirt is missing.

And then I know so much more. Suddenly I'm drowning in memories that take on half shapes. They fill me with panic as I founder around in them.

I know my name: Madison Stanton. I remember my mother, her deep red hair; my father, tall and playful, with a baritone that rumbles comfortingly; my house and its smell of eucalyptus; school; teachers; my best friend, Sandra; my older sister, Kristen; my pet cat, Cozy; and—oh, God— Gabriel. Gabriel whose sweatshirt I am about to lose. All these memories threaten to pull me under a tide of grief and loss.

It is the sound of my own laughter that acts as a life jacket. I float up out of the memories to focus on this moment, on myself standing at that sink. I'm laughing with Sandra. I can't remember what about, though. I'm tempted to move closer.

But first I need to go rescue the sweatshirt. It's about to be stolen. And I know by whom. I left it on the back of a chair—so I wouldn't get paint on it—over on the other side of the partition that divides the room. If I can get to the sweatshirt before Dana does, maybe I can keep her from stealing it.

I try to move toward the partition but have trouble figuring out how to do it. I don't quite have a body, so the physics of movement as I'm used to it on Earth just isn't happening. But I'm also not merely a collection of light particles the way I've gotten used to being back in *Is*. Great. How many different states of existence can there be?

I have to figure out how to use some bizarre combination of floating and running to move. Just as I reach the partition, though, I bounce backward. Rubber-band style. The elastic that holds me to my real self over at the sink has stretched too thin. I go shooting backward almost all the way to the real me over at the sink, who's still busy laughing. What's the matter with her? Or should I say "me"? How am I supposed to refer to the living, breathing Maddy Stanton? "Her" seems so not "me." And yet, she's not me. She doesn't even seem to sense that I'm here. And how am I supposed to let her know she's being clueless about what Dana's doing on the other side of the wall?

I try again to reach Dana, to stop her from stealing the sweatshirt. No luck. The living Maddy pulls me up short once again, only this time I get too close to her. She exerts some kind of magnetic pull on me. And then instantly I *become* her.

age 17

The water suddenly gets too hot on my hands. "Aiya!" I shriek, reaching to adjust the temperature.

Sandra turns the water off. Ever the conservationist. "You're not Lady Macbeth trying to wash bloody sins off your hands, you know."

So Sandra. Thirty seconds ago, we were laughing about the way her calc teacher got a piece of toilet paper stuck in the waist of her skirt, then came to class and taught half the hour without ever realizing it was there. Now Sandra's making obscure references to Shakespearean tragedies.

She hands me the roll of paper towels sitting on the counter, flicking water in my face at the same time. "Thanks," I say, rolling my eyes.

"Sorry," she says, grinning.

We head back over to the table where we've left all our stuff. Time to put Gabe's sweatshirt back on. It smells wonderful. Totally him. I've had it for two days. He left it at my house on Sunday, and I've been making good use of it ever since. Yesterday he asked for it back. Uh-unh. No way. He's not getting it back until it's so dirty it absolutely has to be washed. No use keeping it after it's lost the essential Essence of Gabriel.

It's been a good few days. I'm thinking about raiding Gabe's dirty laundry when I have to give this sweatshirt back.

But when Sandra and I return to the table, the sweatshirt isn't there. My book bag is still sitting on the seat of the chair—exactly where I left it. The sweatshirt should be on the back of the same chair. I glance quickly at the other chairs around the table, but it's not sitting on the back of any of them, either.

"What's wrong?" Sandra asks as I start doing a weird version of Duck Duck Goose with all the chairs, sliding each out and checking to see if the sweatshirt has somehow migrated onto its seat.

"Gabe's sweatshirt is missing," I tell her. I'm not holding out a lot of hope that she's going to sympathize with the true extent of this tragedy. She's been teasing me for the past two days about how my obsession with the sweatshirt is my subconscious attempt to have sex with Gabe.

"It can't be missing," she says matter-of-factly. "It was on the back of the chair when we went to wash our hands."

I'm cursing myself. I took off the sweatshirt so I wouldn't

get paint on it. What's a little paint, though, when the alternative is no sweatshirt at all? I've moved on to playing Duck Duck Goose with the other tables.

No sweatshirt.

There's only one explanation for what could have happened to it. Dana.

Suddenly I'm so angry that I'm afraid I might turn into Lady Macbeth with some bloody sins to wash off my hands after all.

Sandra sees how upset I am. She grabs me by the arm. "Hey, Maddy, it'll turn up."

"Dana took it. I'm sure she did. I don't know whether to be mad that she's trying to mess with me and Gabe, or creeped out by what she might be planning to do with it."

"What do you mean, 'do with it'? What can she do with it?"

I notice that Sandra isn't trying to reassure me that Dana hasn't taken it.

"What if she's going to sleep in it or something?!"

"You mean like you do?"

Such. A. Cheap. Shot. "He's *my* boyfriend," I say defensively. I can't even begin to express how horrified I am by the idea of Gabe's ex sleeping in his sweatshirt. "She can't get over the fact that they've broken up, and I'm sick of it."

Sandra starts rubbing my arm. "Hey, calm down. She's not going to sleep in it. She's over Gabe."

Hardly. She's been a major pain ever since he dumped her and started dating me.

Sandra has known me since we were five. She can see what I'm thinking. That's why it's worth having a best friend. Saves on words. "Seriously," she tells me, "this thing between the two of you, it's about you and her, not about Gabe. She doesn't want *him* back. She just wants to mess with you. It gives her satisfaction to make you miserable because you made her miserable when you started dating him."

I give her my best skeptical look.

She steps back, flicks her brown curly hair over her shoulder. This is a sign she means serious business. The hands even go on her hips. She's got one of those fragile, thin builds (and, yes, I've been envious of that ever since we were about ten and the differences in our body types became clear to me), but she can generate presence when she wants to be taken seriously. Like now. "What better way to upset you than to take something of Gabe's from you? Then she gets to watch you go off."

Sandra nods her head over toward where Dana is standing with some other girls. Dana's smirking in a way that—if I'm honest—actually scares me. How can someone have the look of a jack-o'-lantern *and* a model all at once? "Look at her," Sandra says. "She doesn't have the sweatshirt, so she obviously hid it somewhere around here."

"But where? That means I can find it."

Sandra shakes her head at me. "Don't give her the satisfaction. She's watching you right now to see what you're going to do. Come back after school or something and ask Mrs. Sinclair if you can look around for it then."

The bell rings, and Sandra drags me toward the door.

Suddenly I am ripped away from myself, thrown back into the abyss . . . formless again, isolated in a place that just *Is*. There's the sweatshirt, glowing mockingly at me, reminding me it's no substitute for what's really missing.

the bracelet

THOSE OBJECTS OF LIGHT . . . I know now what they all are: items I lost during my lifetime. They have found their way here, to return me to my own life, and—ohmygod—do I *ever* want to go back.

It's strange that in the art room when I became the living me, she never seemed to realize there was . . . well, another me—a dead one—hanging around somewhere. But in a way it was also nice she didn't notice me. When I became her, it meant I was truly . . . alive.

I want that experience again. I want to be with the people I loved. To see the things that were part of my everyday life. To find out more about who I was. I can remember parts, but not all, of my past. And, as I float here aimlessly in *Is*, I'm already forgetting more about my life.

Now. I want to go back to my life again. Now.

I propel myself through the vacuum of *Is*, looking for something else that will take me home. The closest item to me is the bracelet, so I move straight toward it.

There it is. A ring of light. A phantom wrist longs to feel that bracelet encircling it, longs for the soft tinkling of silver against silver, for the cool brush of chain link against skin.

Knowledge again tears through me. This time, as I scatter through space and darkness, I am sucked toward wind and heat, toward ticklish grass.

I am directly under a tree I have climbed many times with Sandra. I look up into the branches above me, and there she is. An eight-year-old Sandra. Curly dark pigtails ride behind her in the breeze as she maneuvers her way up the tree limbs. And that little girl next to her . . . is me.

Sort of. I recognize my face and crooked teeth from old photos. But it's hard to believe that I ever moved so quickly, or with such freedom. I'm bossing Sandra around, telling her to climb one branch higher. Nothing but this moment seems to exist to that eight-year-old me. She's cast an almost magic spell of oblivion around the whole tree.

As the younger me reaches for a higher branch, sunlight glints off a bracelet dangling from my wrist. The way the sun enchants the charms on that bracelet is fascinating. Tinker Bell, a kitty cat, a ladybug, a silver star . . .

I can remember the bracelet now. It was a gift from my mother for my eighth birthday, and I lost it one day while playing . . . here in Sandra's backyard.

I'm figuring out how this whole object-to-life business seems to be working: see the object I lost in life, imagine using it, go back to the moment I lost it. I just have to say, this seems like a particularly cruel joke. I mean, why all the focus on loss? Isn't losing my life enough? Why is my only option for returning to Earth centered on *losing* something?

As I watch eight-year-old Sandra and myself, I remember the temperature—mild with a forceful wind trying to drive spring into our midst. Earthy spring scents float in my memory, too, mingling with the feel of rough bark against my hands. Sandra and I are daring each other to move as far as we can toward the end of a branch. We are about to—

Fall.

And Sandra is about to break her arm.

I have to do something to stop this from happening. I need to get Sandra's father.

I attempt that strange floating and running movement to get to the house, but, just like the last time I tried it, I discover I'm not allowed to travel far from the living me. I try to stretch the thread of energy that connects the two of us. I strain against it like a dog trying to lengthen its leash enough to reach a taunting squirrel.

No luck. I'm only allowed any kind of freedom of movement if I stay close enough to the living me to see and hear her. She won't even let me get far enough away to help her best friend.

Once again, the Universe's rules for this game suck.

Just as I realize this, the tree branch cracks under the combined weight of two eight-year-olds. We crash through branches, screaming as we fall. I land flat on my stomach. Despite all the years that have passed since this moment, despite even death, I can remember the feel of the air being forced from my lungs as I struggle to breathe.

I can't help running back to try to help these two little girls somehow, but I get too close to the living me. She sucks me in. . . .

age 8

My jaws have slammed together with a force that leaves my head spinning. Blood is warming my mouth as it oozes from a cut, but it takes me a moment to realize this because I still can't breathe.

Sandra is deathly silent. Is she dead?

Now that I can breathe, I scream hysterically.

The back door opens, and Sandra's mother comes

running. She stumbles over to Sandra. She falls down next to her and sobs. "What have you done to her? What have you done to her?"

I try to take in enough air to speak and manage to squeak out, "We fell from the tree. I didn't mean to hurt her."

Mrs. Simpson is breathing all funny. I've never heard anyone breathe like that. What if she and Sandra *both* die? It will be my fault.

Mr. Simpson runs up to us. He tries to get to Sandra, but Mrs. Simpson just keeps crying and breathing all funny and won't let him touch either of them.

I want to help him pull Mrs. Simpson away. What if Sandra's dying and Mrs. Simpson won't let us help her?

"You must calm down, Genevieve," Mr. Simpson keeps telling her. "You'll have an asthma attack."

Will an asthma attack kill Mrs. Simpson?

He's shaking her and pulling her away from Sandra all at once. There's finally a space big enough between Mrs. Simpson and Sandra for him to get into. He kneels by Sandra, leans over her, touches her neck, and listens to her breathing. He makes a strange sound. I think he might be choking on relief. "Sandra'll be fine, but you have to calm down, Genevieve."

I'm relieved that Sandra is going to be all right. If Mr. Simpson says she's okay, then she is. I *like* Mr. Simpson.

I just don't like *Mrs.* Simpson. And now that I know

Sandra is going to be okay, it's fine with me if Mrs. Simpson dies of an asthma attack. Well . . . unless Sandra thinks it's my fault her mom dies.

I want *my* mom. She can make things better. She doesn't have asthma, and she doesn't yell the way Sandra's mom does.

I want my mom *now*.

Where is my magic charm bracelet? I reach for it on my wrist, but it's not there. Where is it? Did all this bad stuff happen because I lost it?

I want to cry but don't dare.

"Genevieve," Mr. Simpson says, "you have to go to the house and call 911."

"I thought you said she'd be okay," she protests.

Mr. Simpson whips around on her in anger. "Dammit, just go call 911," he growls. I want to cheer.

"I can't b-b-breathe," Mrs. Simpson says, gasping.

Mr. Simpson closes his eyes. He looks just like Mom when she's counting to ten as she's ordering me to go to my room to "think about what you've done." When Mr. Simpson opens his eyes, he touches Sandra's cheek lightly—like my dad touches mine at bedtime. Then he stands up and rubs Mrs. Simpson's arms to calm her. When he speaks, his voice is gentle and firm. "She'll probably be fine, Genevieve, but we can't risk moving her ourselves. Go call. Now."

Mrs. Simpson stumbles away. I crawl around, looking

for the bracelet. Now that she's gone, I let the tears stream down my face, but I try to hide them from Mr. Simpson.

He turns to me and sees the tears. "Are you all right, Maddy?" he asks me. "Do you hurt anywhere?"

Everywhere, I want to say, *but mostly just in my heart.* Instead, I say, "I'm okay," but not because I am. I'm terrified, but I can't admit it because I can tell Mr. Simpson isn't really thinking about me, and I don't want him to have to.

"So is Sandra, I think," he tells me reassuringly. "There's a giant goose egg on the side of her head. I think she's just been knocked unconscious. Happened to me once when I was a kid. Looks like her arm might be broken, too, but I think she'll be okay." He starts feeling gently along her other limbs. Then he calls into the house, as if he's surprised to have thought about it, "Genevieve, call Maddy's mom. She'll have to come pick her up. We can't leave Madison here by herself while we're off at the hospital."

Mommy. She'll make everything okay again. I know she will.

Mrs. Simpson has just started out the door. She gives me a mean look, and the screen door slams shut as she moves back into the house. I don't quite understand why she has never liked me.

Mr. Simpson coos gently to his daughter, sparing me a glance as I begin turning in circles. "What are you looking for, Maddy?" he asks me.

"Nothing," I say, even though it's not true.

Mrs. Simpson returns to Sandra's side, crying. And when Sandra's eyes flutter open, Mrs. Simpson squeals in delight. I feel the same way, but my glee has to flutter around inside where it can't be seen or heard. I don't dare draw Mr. and Mrs. Simpson's attention away from Sandra. She's alive. And groaning. In pain.

Time passes, and flashing lights speed up the road toward the house. I recognize my mother's car right behind them. She stays out of the paramedics' way, trailing behind them to the backyard, looking for me. She sees me, runs toward me, pulls me away from all the action, kneels down in front of me and wraps me in her arms.

My mom. She smells like apples: sharp, sweet, and natural. "Are you all right, honey?" she asks.

Now that she's here, the tears turn to sobs. I don't have to hold anything back. But the words I'm trying to say can't be understood, so Mom just keeps reassuring me, "Sandra's okay. She was just knocked unconscious."

Finally, I am able to get out the words clearly, "I can't find my charm bracelet."

She squeezes me tighter. "Shh," she whispers into my ear. "As soon as they've all left with Sandra, we'll look for it."

If she's going to help me look for it, I know we'll find it. She always makes everything all right.

I swallow my sobs and try to breathe deeply.

The paramedics carry Sandra off on a stretcher, and Mom takes me by the hand. We walk in circles around the tree Sandra and I were climbing until . . . finally . . . there it is . . . broken but shining against the grass. Mom picks up the bracelet and lovingly holds it out to me. The second its cool metal touches my skin—

I am gone. Ripped from myself. Thrown back into the abyss . . . formless again, wandering around in a place that just *Is*. I want my mom back. I want to see her again.

My longing to touch her, to be with her, is even greater than the ache I was left with after my first trip back to life.

the purse

THE FEEL OF MY MOM'S ARMS around me has awakened a hunger beyond any I've ever experienced.

I wade back through *Is*, looking for the bracelet. I want to return to that scene in Sandra's backyard. I want to feel my mother's arms around me again—even if it means watching Sandra fall all over again. I refind each of the objects I have encountered before—all except for the bracelet. It's gone.

Strange.

The sweatshirt is still here.

The bracelet isn't.

Loss again. I want to scream, but . . . I don't have a voice.

Is there any other object here that might lead me to my mother? I return to them one at a time, looking for a clue about which will take me where I want to go, but I can't remember where I lost these various scraps of existence. There are the keys, but I don't think they will take me to her. The cell phone's in the next pocket of space. No, that's not a gateway to my mother, either.

Then there's the purse. It hums and glows more intensely than the other objects do when I get close to it.

Is it connected to my mother? I don't think so, but I can't help feeling drawn in by the intensity of the object's presence. I want the answers it seems to be offering. Maybe those answers will ultimately lead me back to my mother . . . and everything else I want to reach. I muster every phantom feeling I can to remember carrying a purse. And once again those powerful feelings rip through me. I am propelled toward something . . . unpleasant.

I'm in an uncomfortable, stuffy environment, surrounded by the scent of urine. I realize I am in a bathroom stall at Overton High School. An alive and seventeen-year-old me is entering through the bathroom door, getting closer to me, and I am . . . sucked in.

When a girl has to pee, she really has to pee. I slam the door of the stall behind me and dump my purse—unusually heavy today with all the extra change in it—on top of the roll of toilet paper.

It falls off. Gross. Who knows what this floor has had on it? Taking a pee will just have to wait until I pick it up. Why was I stupid enough to bring it with me?

I'm just putting it back when voices bounce off the tiles of the bathroom wall. I recognize Tammy Havers's voice. "Anyone in here?" she asks someone.

"I don't think so," comes the reply.

So I'm just unbuckling my belt when Tammy demands payment from the mystery voice. I realize what's happening on the other side of the stall door: Tammy is selling drugs.

Damn.

Peeing is going to have to wait. I don't dare make any noise right now.

Apparently not making any noise is one of those "easier said than done" things. Especially if you're stupid enough to set your favorite purse on top of a roll of toilet paper for a second time and you then back into it. And if said purse has about three dollars in coins in it because you're stupid enough to have lost your lunch debit card . . . well, it hits the floor with a pretty loud thud.

The kind of thud that alerts the drug dealer there's someone else in the bathroom.

Tammy wouldn't kick in the stall door or anything, would she?

And why exactly couldn't this have happened—if it *had* to happen at *all*—after I'd already gone pee? I'm dying here.

Tammy pushes on the stall door and finds it latched. "Come out of there," she demands.

"Uh, no, thanks," I say.

Fortunately, she doesn't try to force it open.

*Un*fortunately, she crawls *under* the partition on the left, knocking my purse into the next stall.

If I'd had any brains, I'd have realized sooner that my incredibly heavy-with-change purse would make a good weapon. I'd have already picked it up and smacked her on the head with it, hopefully knocking her out. Now it's too far away for me to reach.

I guess it doesn't matter anyway. The truth is I wouldn't have actually hurt Tammy. I mean, she and I were friends until eighth grade. And not only wouldn't I go whacking her over the head, but I can't believe she'd truly hurt me, either.

Well, other than torturing me by sending me to another bathroom to pee. Ohmygod, would I even make it at this point?

And wasting time thinking about all this has now left me completely at Tammy's mercy, because there she is. Standing in the stall with me. Glaring at me.

She unlatches the door, grabs me by the hair, and yanks me out of the stall. I want to scream in pain. It really hurts. But I'm too afraid to do anything more than gasp. So much for old friendship protecting me from Tammy's wrath.

"What are you doing in here, Stanton?" She yanks on my hair for emphasis.

If she yanks on it again, I swear she'll unleash a puddle of pee right beneath us.

"I asked you a question," Tammy says. "What are you doing in here?"

Duh. Going to the bathroom, perhaps? But I don't exactly want to make Tammy any angrier than she already is, so I try the less sarcastic approach. "I'm just going to the bathroom."

"Did you hear anything?"

"Hear what?"

Tammy yanks again. Is she waiting for me to confess? Bravado might be my only way out. "Why are you trying to torture me?" I ask, reminding myself that I've known Tammy since we were in preschool.

We were never great friends when we were younger, but we always got along. Then in fourth grade, neither of us had any really close friends in our class, so we ended up eating lunch together every day. We even shared Twinkies.

She only started getting messed up when we were in middle school. Something went down at home, and she started getting tougher and tougher. I was sad when it happened. I liked her. But she wouldn't talk to me about what was going on.

Then, in eighth grade, after the whole Ouija board thing that happened at my sleepover, she stopped talking to me altogether. Thought I was making fun of her. But I swear I wasn't.

By the end of eighth grade, she started getting downright scary. Once I even saw her beat the crap out of some kid during lunch. I wasn't exactly valiant or anything. No saving the kid, jumping in front of her with fists at the ready. No. I was one of the cowards watching the whole thing. Besides, you couldn't really get in between the two girls. Even then, Tammy liked grabbing the hair of her opponent. When the teachers came to break up the fight, Tammy almost ripped the other kid's scalp right off her head while the adults were trying to separate the two of them.

Now, I realize, is not the time to be remembering that Jenny Wilson almost became a scalpless wonder. Think Twinkies, I tell myself. The image of a ten-year-old Tammy stuffing yellow cream-filled pastries in her mouth does help me face off against her. Even if the hair-grip is still killing me.

As she yanks even harder, I opt for the remember-when-we-were-friends approach. "Okay. Jesus. Let go of my hair. I did hear what was happening in here, but it's not like I'm gonna *tell* anyone. Get real. We've known each other for ages, Tammy. It's not as if I'm going to rat on someone I used to share Twinkies with at lunch."

"You'd better not," Tammy says. She gives my hair a threatening reminder of her willingness to hurt me. "'Cause if I get ratted on, I'm gonna know exactly who to blame."

Adults are always wanting you to tell in a situation like this. *We can protect you. It's for the good of everyone. Blah, blah, blah.*

Right. Adults are *so* stupid. I can't figure out how they managed to live long enough to survive high school.

"I'm not going to say anything," I tell Tammy. I hope I sound firm, disgusted at the mere possibility. But I hear a squeak in my voice. She finally lets go of my hair, pushing me away from her at the same time. "Get out of here."

"Umm . . . could I, like, just get my money first?"

She freezes me with this what-kind-of-an-idiot-*are*-you stare.

Okay, then. Guess I'll just borrow money from Sandra for lunch. I want to kick myself. I wouldn't need to borrow money from my best friend if I'd just admitted to my mother that I'd lost the lunch card. She'd have gotten me a new one. But I didn't want to listen to her harping about how I can never hold on to anything . . . which is irritatingly true, I realize, as I practically run the rest of the way from the bathroom. And that's when . . .

Is embraces me again.

I float for a moment, just remembering what it was like to be Maddy Stanton. It seems that I have found the corner pieces of a jigsaw puzzle, but I am still trying to find all the edges. My life is lying in a heap of memories piled on top of one another, small clips of partial images carved into funny shapes. They aren't even sorted yet. Which piece do I even start trying to build from?

Of course . . .

The one with the Grim Reaper on it. The one that tells me how I died. But I don't know where it is yet. I might have to turn over a lot of pieces before I'm likely to even catch a fragment of the Reaper's image.

It's time to start now.

I find the purse. If that and the sweatshirt are still here in *Is*, why can't I find the charm bracelet? I wade off in search of the bracelet once again.

Still gone.

What is the difference between the charm bracelet and the purse? Between the sweatshirt and the charm bracelet?

And then I know.

The real me, the alive me . . . she took the bracelet with

her when she left the scene where I saw her. But the purse and the sweatshirt . . . I didn't find either of those before I left the scene. Who knows what ever happened to them? But somehow I never got them back, and so here they are in *Is*, still haunting me.

An idea hums through me: Perhaps if I don't find the object, I can return to the moment I lost it, but if I do find it, then I can't get back to that time.

Control.

I might have some control over what moments in my life I can return to. I just have to keep myself from finding something.

But wait. I don't know for certain this is how it works. . . .

Or even if I can change what happens when I return to a moment.

I realize there's a way to find out.

I wade my way back to the purse and imagine myself holding it again.

The stuffiness of an enclosed bathroom, the scent of urine, myself walking toward me . . . it's all there again. I embrace myself, and we join fluidly. . . .

I *so* have to pee.

I set my purse on top of the roll of toilet paper, but it falls off. Disgusting. This floor could have had—well, who knows what—on it. I'm bending over to pick up the purse when I realize I'm feeling that funny thing again. It's happened to me a couple times before. I can't explain the feeling. It's like I'm being spied on. It's creepy. I tried to explain it to my mom once, and she told me she'd had creepy feelings like that before, too. Said she'd felt "someone walking over her grave." Like that makes sense?

Unfortunately, at the moment, it does.

Shake it off, I tell myself.

I set the bag back on the roll of toilet paper and look around, like I'm expecting to see a ghost here or something. How stupid is *that*?

"Anyone in here?" someone says through the bathroom door. I know that voice. It belongs to Tammy Havers.

"I don't think so," someone replies.

Tammy demands payment.

Great. A drug deal. I pause in unbuckling my belt . . . I so have to pee, but self-preservation? Yeah. Might be more important at the moment. I think I'll just try not to make any sound. . . .

Thunk.

My bag. The one with about three dollars in change in it. Why did I have to lose my lunch debit card?

I really have to pee.

Someone pushes on the stall door. Tammy, I'm pretty sure, because now she's also demanding that I come out of there.

"Uh, no, thanks," I say. That creepy shivery feeling comes over me again. Must be because Tammy is crawling under the stall now. I look around for my purse. As heavy as it is, it might even make a good weapon at the moment.

I can't find it. Who knows where it landed?

Then Tammy is there, standing in front of me with this totally killer glare.

She opens the stall door, grabs a handful of my hair, and tugs me out. This is *way* too much. That creepy feeling invading me, Tammy abusing me, majorly having to pee, and being *interrupted* . . . how much does a girl have to put up with?

"What are you doing in here, Stanton?" She yanks on my hair again for emphasis.

It's like my hair is a pull-string attached to my bladder. If Tammy pulls on it again, I think she'll unleash a tidal wave of pee.

"I asked you a question," Tammy says. "What are you doing in here?"

"What do you think I'm doing?" I ask, my anger

overflowing. "I'm taking a pee. Or at least I was trying to."

"Did you hear anything?" She starts to pull on my hair again.

"Don't!" I tell her. "Of course I heard you. But it's not like I'm gonna tell anyone about it. Get real. We've known each other for ages, Tammy. And even if I do think it's kind of stupid to be taking drugs, and even *stupider* to be dealing them here at school—like, have you heard the word *expulsion*?—I'm hardly going to rat on someone I used to share Twinkies with at lunch."

She seems to give this some thought. "You'd better not. 'Cause if I get ratted on, I'm gonna know who to blame."

"I'm not going to say anything. Trust me." Thank God I don't sound like I'm begging.

"Get out of here," Tammy says.

She lets go of my hair. I dash into the stall.

"What are you doing?" Tammy asks in disbelief as I begin searching under the partitions between the stalls.

"Looking for my stupid money." I find it just inside the adjoining stall.

"Just get the hell out of here," Tammy says.

"On my way," I say. I grab the purse—

Back in *Is*, I search, propelling myself through miles of space, looking for the purse.

It's gone. Just like the bracelet. The moment I touched

each, I was ripped away from life and returned to *Is*.

Then how did I get back to *Is* from the moments when I didn't find the objects? I reflect on the sweatshirt incident, then try to compare it to the first purse one. But I can't.

In fact, I can't recall *anything* that happened the first time I went into that bathroom. The second experience with that moment has wiped out the first. It has become the new reality of my life.

Is seems to work on a different plane of reality, though, because I can remember the decision that I made to go back and change that scene. So while I know there was a time when I didn't find the handbag, that time has disappeared forever.

In a way, this is pretty cool. It means I can make some conscious choices about how to change my life.

But—changing my life so I find an object just seems to make it impossible for me to go back to that moment. Why would I want to do *that*?

Will it work the other way around? Can I *keep* myself from finding something?

Probably . . . not.

Wouldn't I have to know—when I was looking for it—that I didn't actually want to find the object? Since I can't remember where the object will take me (or why and how I lost it) until I've used it to go back to life, that would mean I'd have to find the object, get sent back to *Is*, and realize I wish I'd never found the object.

By then, the object would already be gone from *Is*.

The Universe isn't nearly as generous as I thought it was.

Or maybe I'm not supposed to be messing around with my original life that way.

I can't quite explain what's happened now that I have changed the outcome in finding my purse, but something's different. About me. About my life.

About who I am.

And I'm not sure I like it.

When I went back and made myself find that purse, I somehow became a new person. Someone who—first of all—could sense that I was there. That must have been what the creepy feeling was. My intention to change what happened in that moment somehow changed everything. I knew I was there. Well, kind of, anyway. Enough to make the moment feel . . . spooky.

But that's not all. Other things changed, too. I just don't know what they are. If I never found my purse in the first version of my life, did I go without lunch that day? Did I borrow money from someone else so I could eat? I have no way of knowing, but whatever happened in that first version created a different life than did the results of my second visit to that moment.

Even being back here in *Is* feels different than it did before. I'm a whole different *dead* person than I was.

It's hard to describe what all this has done to me, but it's as if I were listening to a song and when I got back it was playing in a different key. Everything jumped up a half note . . . or something like that.

Who knows what I could be messing with going around and changing the way things happened in life?

Suppose I could keep myself from dying?

But I can't possibly know which of these moments can lead to that outcome. At least at this point.

And what if I end up making myself die sooner?

Making decisions in death doesn't seem to be any easier than making them in life: You never know what the outcome is going to be one way or the other.

$$\boxed{\text{orchids}}$$

I MISS EVERYTHING about being real. Using these objects to return to life . . . it's like an addiction. I have to have another fix. I just can't decide which object to use next. The keys, buttons, beads, pen, Barbie doll, key chain . . .

In the end, I don't actually get a choice. I come across some orchids, eerie, almost skeletal in their luminescent form, and before I know it, I'm remembering that I wore them in my hair for my sister's wedding. The memory is enough to carry me home, to the moment when . . .

I am on my knees in the grass, dark night surrounding me. Gabriel is standing next to me, bent over at the waist, his hand firmly gripping my upper arm.

"Try breathing deeply," Gabriel urges me.

It sounds like a good idea, but I'm gulping more than I'm breathing, and the extra air I'm taking in is making me feel sicker, not better.

It has been an incredibly long day. I'm now convinced I'll never consider having a wedding. If I ever want to get married, I'll elope. What could Kristen have been thinking?

Her wedding dress was beautiful, but how could she have dressed me in this horrible, full-length strapless dress? If she was going to make me be a bridesmaid (let's not kid ourselves; I had no choice in this; Mom would have killed me if I hadn't agreed to do it—or, worse yet, she might have yammered on for days at a time about the importance and meaning of family, about my lifetime relationship with my older sister, etc.), why did she have to put me in such a long dress? I've lived in fear all day of tripping over the hem of the gown. That walk down the aisle? Nightmare. I almost stumbled. And how humiliating, having to walk down the aisle on the arm of Gabriel—one of the most gorgeous guys at school, and cousin to the groom! His firm grip on my arm kept me from making a complete fool of myself in front of everyone in the church, but he obviously noticed my clumsiness. He winked at me and everything. Winked! Ohmygod. So unfair. Why couldn't I have walked down the aisle with the groom's brother instead? I mean, he is, like, thirty, so no attraction there, right? And he'd probably have pretended not to notice that I was a complete klutz.

To make it all worse, a few days ago Gabriel broke up with his girlfriend, Dana (who'd been his girlfriend for, like, *two years*). I haven't been able to stop thinking about that all day long. It's the kind of thing that, you know, gives a girl a glimmer of hope—as if I had a chance with a guy as hot as Gabe Archer.

Sandra's always telling me that I'm prettier than I think I am—that my freckles are cute and that my brown hair has just the right red highlights, but she's my best friend, so she has to say stuff like that. It's not as if a few halfway decent features will attract a guy who has absolutely everything going for him. He's friendly, smart, and has these wide, wide shoulders that fill out his tux perfectly. . . .

I've been tormenting myself with thoughts like this all day. My mom hasn't made getting Gabe off my mind any easier, either. She's reminded me—like, seven times—about the crush I had on Gabe back when I was in sixth grade.

Back then, *every* girl crushed on Gabe. He had this

butter-blond hair that curled into perfect ringlets. He was shorter than I was, but I had dreams of him shooting past me in height. My mother laughed the first time she saw him and figured out how I felt about him.

But she's not laughing anymore. In the years since then, Gabe has obliged me by growing a lot. He's a couple inches past six feet now. His hair has darkened some over the years, but it's still a shade of blond. The curls are gorgeous, too. I'd kill to have hair that beautiful. And his shoulders have filled out.

So, last night, at the wedding rehearsal when Mom saw him for the first time since sixth grade, she was surprised by how much he'd changed. She's been telling me ever since how lucky I am to get to walk up the aisle with such an "attractive" (totally her word, *not* mine) young man. The job included the responsibility of being his partner during the second dance of the evening, too. And I admit the idea had a lot of appeal.

Until right between the wedding and the reception— which is when I started to feel not so hot. I didn't want to say anything about it to my mom. I mean, what could she do? She was busy being the mother of the bride. And I wouldn't want to ruin Kristen's wedding, either.

I thought at first that I was just tired. It'd been a long morning and afternoon. So I just kept trying to muddle through. By the time dinner arrived at the table, my eyeballs felt like they were on fire. I started wondering if I had a fever.

Gabe was sitting next to me. "You don't look so great, Maddy," he told me.

Gee . . . just what every girl wants some hot guy to say to her. He realized his mistake right away, and he started stuttering, "I mean—not that way, just, you know . . . like you don't feel so good. You look great in that dress and all . . . y'know. I just meant you . . . are you sick?"

The sound of concern in his voice cheered me up a little but not much. "I don't know," I told him. "Let's hope not."

We were sitting on a dais at the head table—facing all the other wedding guests. He glanced out at the crowd of faces. "Yeah, let's hope not," he said. He dove into his food with an enthusiasm that made me feel even sicker. The sounds all around me were ringing in my head, too. All that cheering, and the frequent clinking of knives on champagne glasses . . . *way* too much for me.

"Ummm, I think I'd better get out of here," I said to Gabe. "Will you tell Her Highness that I think I'm going to be sick? Otherwise, she's sure to raise hell about my leaving right now." Her Highness was Brenda Jackson, my sister's college roommate, maid of honor, and Manager Extraordinaire. I'd been bossed around by her so much in the past few weeks that I was ready to kill her.

Gabe hadn't had as many opportunities to run afoul of

her, but last night she'd been so bossy that even he'd commented on it. That's when I shared with him my nickname for her.

Gabe's mouth was full, but he nodded his head vigorously and then started to stand up as if he were planning to come with me. Right. Gabe in the ladies' restroom. Not such a good idea. I held my hand up, and he stopped midmove. Then I turned and fled from the dais and toward the bathrooms.

Just my luck, there were, like, twenty women in there, going to the bathroom or refreshing their makeup.

I turned and ran outside, looking for an inconspicuous spot where I could have some privacy. I could barely stand up.

And then Gabe was there, holding on to my arm. By that point, I was glad he'd followed me, because I didn't think I could stand on my own anymore. I sank onto my knees.

Now he's holding me tightly against him so I don't do a complete nose-dive into the grass. I wobble a bit and my hair brushes against his chest. Some of it is pulled out of its updo. The orchids from my hair tumble to the ground between us.

He has just gotten down on his knees beside me and is telling me to try breathing deeply. We hear Her Highness's voice coming at us across the lawn. "What's wrong with her, Gabe?"

I groan. "Does she have to yell loud enough for the whole world to hear?" I ask, just as my body begins to shudder. I want to throw up, but with Gabe here, I want even more desperately not to humiliate myself in front of him.

Unfortunately, millions of years of evolution, designed to help humans combat viruses and food poisoning, causes my stomach to callously disregard the needs of my self-esteem.

My stomach erupts.

The disgusting taste of bile fills my mouth, and Brenda's voice reaches me from the background: "Hold her up, Gabriel! Hold her up! She's going to soil her dress."

Even as I lose the contents of my stomach, a part of my brain is capable of wondering who ever talks about *soiling* a dress. Soiling? I mean, come on.

But that thought is quickly replaced by the realization that something horrendous—even more horrendous than barfing in front of a hot guy—is happening. Gabriel is trying to hold me up enough to keep me from "soiling" my dress, but he has forgotten a key law of physics:

> The force exerted on **Object One** (my shoulders) + the force exerted on **Object Two** (my strapless dress, which is trapped beneath my knees) = **mortification** (when my dress does not follow my shoulders upward, but my breasts do).

Her Highness has arrived and seems to realize this situation requires the Maneuvering of an Expert (this is the first time I have ever been thankful for Brenda's bossiness). She pushes Gabe away from me (So what if I fall face-forward into my own barf? Way less embarrassing than leaving my chest exposed) and starts stuffing me back into my dress while yelling at Gabe, "Get out of here! Go! Go get her mother!"

Gabe disappears, my stomach stops ejecting its contents, and Brenda is ripping up pieces of grass. She uses them to try to wipe my face and mouth. I'd prefer to "soil" the hem of my dress, but Brenda sees what I'm trying to do and manhandles me into submission. Then she pulls me away from the barf and gently rests me on my side.

"Madison, have you been drinking?"

The very thought makes my stomach revolt all over again. I groan. "Nooo . . . I think I've got the flu. I haven't been feeling so great all day."

She kneels down beside me. "Poor kid," she says, and—as we wait for my mother—pets my hair like I'm a dog.

Mom runs up to us, her violet mother-of-the-bride dress (*Why* do they make those out of such awful material?) fanning out behind her in the breeze.

"Oh, sweetie, what's wrong?" she asks. She takes over petting my hair, but she's had lots of practice at it, so it feels like a mother comforting a daughter. None of that pet-the-dog stuff.

"She thinks she has the flu," Brenda tells her. "She said she hasn't felt well all day."

"You should have said something. I would have figured out how to get you out of this situation," Mom tells me, but not like she's angry or frustrated with me. Just like she wants me to know it would have been okay for me to ask for help.

She guides me to my feet and then encourages me to lean against her as we start to move. "I'm taking you home right now. Brenda, tell Kristen and John where I've gone, and that I'll be back as soon as possible. They'll just have to hold up the bridal dance until I manage to get back."

Mom leads me carefully toward the car. . . .

Now I know. . . . It's getting too far from a lost object, leaving it behind, that launches me back to *Is*. I can't remain indefinitely in my life. The Universe only lets me stay there until I've found the object or moved a certain distance from it.

But, thankfully, it lets me return as many times as I want to a moment if I never find the object.

This makes me glad the flowers have been left behind. I'm able to return and return and return to this moment. The nausea, the vomiting, the humiliation, all of it's worth it to reexperience the feel of Gabriel's grip on my arm when I'm falling, and of Mom's hand gently brushing my hair away from my face when I most need her.

And by the time I've gone through this experience several times, I discover that as long as I'm not trying to change anything while I'm there, the living me doesn't feel that creepy sense of being watched.

Strange, huh?

But here's something even stranger: After about my fourth time visiting this moment, I actually begin to *like* Brenda.

random acts of existence

age 13

I'm digging through a little plastic bag looking for a purple rubber band to attach to my braces. I'm hoping there's one more. I've already put one on the right side. The colors of my rubber bands have to match, right? Green, yellow, red.

I'm standing at the end of a row of lockers, and Sandra, who's supposed to be blocking me from everyone's view, starts to move away. "Hey, get back here," I say. I don't want the whole world to see me digging around in my mouth for the after-lunch-rubber-band-replacement session. What if Paul walks by?

I find a purple rubber band. I reach for it and start to loop it around the hook on my bottom row of braces.

"Ooohhh . . . Oh, nooo!" The disappointment in Sandra's voice distracts me. I pull a little too hard on the rubber band. It snaps and flies out of my mouth.

How humiliating.

Then I see what Sandra's just seen.

Incredible. Awful.

Paul's walking down the hallway with Mary Kramer. And they're holding hands.

Sandra sees the look on my face and reaches out to touch my arm. "I can't believe he'd do that, go back to his ex-girlfriend that way."

Sandra might not be able to believe it, but I can. Mary Kramer is about a million times prettier than I am. She never needs to worry about whether the rubber bands on her braces match because she has the world's most perfect teeth and will never need orthodontics.

Sandra's going on. "Besides, you didn't really like him all that much, did you?"

Past tense. As if I have already *stopped* liking him.

The irony is that Paul was only my boyfriend for two weeks. My first boyfriend. And that's more because he picked me than because I picked him. I didn't even like him two weeks ago when the rumors started going around that he liked me. But I wanted a boyfriend, so I gave him a chance, got to know—and really like—him at Amber's party a week ago. We even kissed in her basement.

And, wow, I guess that was a huge mistake. It was my first kiss and I failed at it. Paul laughed at me and said, "That's not what you do," before trying to teach me the "right" way to kiss—which had something to do with sharing his gum.

I bet Mary Kramer's a better kisser than I am. That's probably the number one reason he's back with her.

And now I'm stuck liking him. Probably forever.

Sandra puts her arm around my shoulders. "He's a jerk. Forget about him. You'll find someone better."

I don't think so. I'm a failure. I'm never going to like a guy again.

Tammy walks by. She sees the look on my face and does a double take. Almost like she wants to say something to me. That would be the first time since the slumber party last month. Maybe she realizes I wasn't trying to make fun of her when we were playing with the Ouija board. I'm hopeful for a second.

Then she's gone.

Lately, it seems like I'm losing everyone I care about.

Sandra leads me away from the lockers and toward our fifth-hour class.

"Kristen, stop hitting your sister," Mom says. We are driving to Florida. I am six, and my parents have promised me a trip to Disney World for spring break. Kristen is too old to enjoy the trip. At thirteen, she'd rather be going somewhere exciting with her friends, but my parents keep reminding her that *she* got to go to Disney World when she was little and now it's my turn.

I grin in satisfaction and say in my head, *You got in trouble, you got in trouble.* I know better than to say it aloud. That will get *me* in trouble with Dad, who is already annoyed. But Kristen can tell I'm making fun of her with my eyes. She knocks a package of Life Savers out of my hand so hard that some of them roll along the floor and under the seat. I start scavenging for them. When I think I have them all, I stick my tongue out at Kristen. She just glares back.

"Turn on the air-conditioning," Kristen moans for at least the twentieth time.

It's not all that hot in the car. We're only in southern Ohio, and it's just the beginning of April. "I'll turn it on when we get farther south and it's hotter," Dad says.

Kristen makes a nasty snorting sound. Dad likes to have the windows of the car open, but the wind whipping through them is messing up Kristen's hair. I just don't see the big deal. Now getting to see Aurora and Belle and Ariel—that will be a *big* deal. I can't think about anything else. I have all my princess books stacked in my lap.

I flip one open and start reading it. "Want to read with me?" I offer Kristen. I can think of no greater peace offering.

She glares at me.

"Please. They're good books."

She rolls her eyes at me and pulls out a pillow, then hides her face underneath it.

Mom sees the hurt look on my face. "Don't worry about it, Maddy," she tells me. "Just enjoy your books."

"Will you read along with me?" I ask. I want company.

Mom smiles at me. "Next rest stop I'll change places with Kristen. She can sit up here, and I'll sit back there with you so we can read the stories together."

"Thank God," Kristen emerges from under the pillow long enough to say. Then she hides back underneath it. The next few minutes are peaceful until Dad stops at the rest area. When we all get out of the car . . .

age 11

I'm in Sandra's bedroom. I'm trying to get dressed and pack my clothes, but I'm missing a pair of socks.

It's Sandra's eleventh birthday, and we were planning to

have a sleepover. *Were* is the most important word here.

Sandra's mother hasn't been feeling well lately, so every time in the past few months we've asked if I could stay over, we've been told no. Sandra's mother suffers from bad migraines. Noise makes them worse. So it makes sense to me that I shouldn't spend the night at her house.

But why Sandra hasn't been able to stay the night at my house . . . that I just don't get. Every time we bring the subject up with her mother, she starts saying things like, "If you really feel you must go, darlin', I understand." Her mother was raised in the South, and she has this honeyed way of speaking the word *darlin'* that drives me crazy; maybe that's because Sandra melts whenever her mother says it. And to make things worse, her mother adds something like, "I'm feeling so sick, darlin', that I can understand why you'd rather be at a friend's house than here keeping me company. But I'll miss you so much while you're gone. Who will bring me my cup of tea when I don't even think I can make it out of bed?"

That just sort of kills any desire Sandra has to stay at my house.

Sandra and I have been fighting about this stuff a lot lately. I keep saying she should stay at my house even though her mother doesn't want her to. She says she just can't, not when her mother needs her so much.

Two days ago, when Sandra invited me to her house for

a birthday sleepover, I was crazy excited. It's been ages since we've spent the night together.

I should have known better. Mrs. Simpson is a master-mind at ruining my time with Sandra, and I should have expected her to pull it off tonight, too. Except I guess I thought that, this being a birthday, her mother would go out of her way to make it a nice night for Sandra.

No such luck.

Five minutes ago, Sandra's mom knocked on the bed-room door, stuck her head inside, and said, "I'm so sorry, girls, but I have a migraine coming on. I'm afraid that Madison is going to have to go home."

"Please, Mom," Sandra begged. "We'll be quiet. I prom-ise. We haven't had a sleepover in ages."

Mrs. Simpson started crying. "I'm so sorry, darling. I wanted so badly for this to be a perfect night for the two of you. Maybe Daddy can take me to a motel so I can have enough quiet to recover. I'd just be so lonely there all by myself. Your dad would have to come back here to check on you. And I get so scared when I'm so sick. I can't get up by myself if I need to. But I'll call Madison's mom and tell her not to come get her if your father says—"

"No, Mom," Sandra said. "We understand. We'll do it again some other time."

Except *I* definitely *don't* understand. I want to cry. I'm feeling ripped apart inside. My best friend isn't really my best friend. *My* best friend wouldn't let her mother do this to her. How can Sandra not see this is all an act on her mother's part? That her mother *wants* to ruin our time together?

Sandra's mother leaves the room, and I look at the devastated expression on Sandra's face. Her brownish-green eyes are wide and glittering. She's holding her own arms like she's hugging herself. Even her normally bouncing, curly hair seems to drag along the side of her face. Guilt washes over me.

None of this is Sandra's fault.

The doorbell rings. My mother is here. I still haven't found my socks. I don't want to leave Sandra here by herself wearing that desperate expression . . . on her *birthday* of all days. But now I can hear my mother's voice in the entryway. She's asking for me. Forget the socks. I know it's a bizarre idea, but I figure that they can stay here and keep Sandra company for the night.

I give Sandra a hug. A sob starts to wrack her body, but as her mother walks back into the room, she chokes it down.

"Bye," I whisper, letting go and rushing from the room.

I pull some books from my locker, and a pen slides out. I try to catch it, but my hands are full. It lands on the floor and makes a rolling escape toward Sandra, who's standing right next to me at her locker. She yanks hard on the handle of the locker's jammed door. It suddenly gives up its fight to protect her books from the odious duty of accompanying her to class. But lockers are not above simple revenge. Books, notebooks, even a pencil case, slide off the top shelf. She jumps back to avoid the avalanche.

I'm laughing at the bizarre look on her face when I hear a voice behind me say, "Hey . . ."

Ohmygod. Go away, I think. Thankfully, I have the presence of mind not to let the idea slip out of my mouth. Nausea rises in my stomach at the sound of Gabe's voice. Must be the memory of Kristen's wedding.

That and the rumor I heard earlier today that he's planning to ask me out.

By the time I turn around, he's helping Sandra pick up the mess on the floor.

"Thanks," she says as he hands her a pile of papers that's fallen out of a book. I'm such an idiot. Why am I standing here instead of helping them?

Useless now. They're done.

Gabe turns toward me. As his eyes meet mine, my

stomach lurches crazily.

Gabe says, "So, I hear Kristen and John get back from the honeymoon in a few days."

I should be able to handle a few sentences of small talk, right?

My eyes skitter away from his, and I look to Sandra for help, but she's kneeling in front of her locker, going through papers on the locker floor. She hasn't bothered to clean anything in there all year. She's obviously trying to eavesdrop.

She's also obviously not going to bail me out.

"Yeah," I say. I'm such a brilliant conversationalist. I scour my brain for things to add to this exchange.

"Hawaii . . . wow, what a great honeymoon."

"Yeah."

"That's an encouraging streak," he says.

"What do you mean?" I ask.

"A couple of 'yeahs' right in a row. Shall I go for another one?"

Dread descends.

"So there's a party this Friday at Allan Redford's house. Want to go with me?"

Yeah, I do. Only I can't say that because I also don't want to go.

Sandra's behind Gabe's back making go-for-it-girl gestures at me.

"Well, actually, I can't. My family has plans and my

mother really expects me to be there. . . ." I can tell from his face that he's not buying it.

"Oh, well, then. Maybe another time?"

I swallow and this time manage, "Yeah." But then feel compelled to add, "Maybe."

Gabe doesn't waste any time getting away from me. "Later, then," he says, and walks away.

I turn to face Sandra. The look she's giving me is even worse than the look my mother gave me when I got caught cheating on a test in fifth grade. "For God's sake, why'd you do that? Are you crazy? You've had a crush on Gabe since, what, like, seventh grade?"

"Sixth," I mumbled.

"Which just makes it worse! What are you thinking?"

"It's just, well . . . it's—I'm not so sure. . . . Well, you know how when you've been eating something right before you get the flu and then every time you even *think* about that kind of food—for, like, the next year—you think you're going to be sick again?"

Sandra looks at me as if I'm crazy. It takes her a minute to put the pieces together. "Wait. Are you trying to tell me that Gabe makes you feel *nauseated*?"

"Uhmm . . . yeah? Well, not exactly him. Just the memory of him at the wedding."

"Oh, for God's sake, Maddy. Take some Pepto-Bismol or something. But get over it. That's the stupidest thing I've ever heard." Sandra slams her locker and glares at me.

I can't quite explain everything to her. She wouldn't understand that Pepto-Bismol might help with the nausea, but it's not going to help with all the other things that are roiling inside me.

Like total embarrassment over falling out of my dress in front of Gabe.

Or fear of picking up a rebound boyfriend and losing him within days—the way I did in eighth grade. Two weeks of going with me was enough to drive Paul back to a girl who'd only been his girlfriend for a couple of months. What chance do I have of keeping a hot guy like Gabe, who's had the same girlfriend for two years? And, okay, so she's one of the witchiest girls I've ever met. Still, she must have some redeeming qualities if Gabe stayed with her that long.

And then there's that awful kiss I shared with Paul back in eighth grade. I've kissed a few boys since then, but no one that I actually liked. They were just guys at a party looking for someone to make out with. What if I kiss Gabe and *he* laughs at me because I'm doing it wrong?

I'd rather be lonely every Friday night for the rest of my life.

But part of me knows that all these things I'm worried about—falling out of my dress, Gabe seeing me throw up, getting laughed at for the way I kiss—these are mostly excuses so I can avoid admitting what the biggest problem is. Change. I hate it. I'm used to my life just like it is. If I'm the girl who just *dreams* about kissing Gabe, then I know exactly who I am.

Sandra begins to walk away. "Wait! Where are you going?" I ask. We always walk to class together.

She gives me an "oh, *please*" look. "You know exactly where I'm going," she says. Then she turns and starts walking again.

She's right. I do know where she's going. She'll catch up with Gabe and tell him not to give up, that he should ask me out again.

Trying to stop her will be useless. I'm both terrified and relieved by the realization.

I close my locker, noticing that my pen is still on the ground. I reach for—

age 7

"Kitty, no!" I shout, just as her little ginger paws land in my carefully sorted piles of beads. Purple, pink, and turquoise beads scatter across the tabletop before pattering onto the floor.

At first, our new kitty is startled by the noise. She jumps backward on the table, bumping into a bowl of fruit. But as the beads continue bouncing across the floor, her ears prick up and fascination gleams in her eyes.

She pounces.

More beads roll across the table and plunge to the floor, followed by the soft plunk of a three-pound kitten chasing them.

"No, no!" I shout again, frantically trying to gather the beads back together. I'm only halfway through the necklace I'm making and if I lose these beads, I won't have enough.

The new kitty is batting at the beads, chasing them around the kitchen. Several roll under the refrigerator. More travel under the stove.

"Stop it, kitty," I moan.

Mom puts her arm around my shoulder. "It's all right, Madison," she tells me. "We'll get them out somehow."

"But what if I don't have enough to finish my necklace?"

Kristen and Dad are now intentionally kicking the beads around the floor, laughing as the cat chases them.

"This is all part of having this cat you've been asking for for months now."

It's true. I've been asking for a cat for a long time. And I was so happy at lunchtime. Tiny, furry, blue-eyed . . . my dreams came true when Mom walked through the door with her.

But now . . . *now* I'm thinking this might be a bad idea. Sure, "hard work" and "responsibility" were mentioned. But no one thought to tell me a kitten would ruin my necklace.

Kristen picks up the kitty, who starts to purr immediately. I'm jealous. She hasn't purred for me yet. "Let me have her," I say.

"In a minute," Kristen says.

"Help me get your beads," Mom says before I can wrestle the cat from Kristen.

Mom grabs a hanger from the closet next to the kitchen and starts sweeping it below the stove. A rainbow of beads emerges, and Mom moves on to sweep the area under the refrigerator.

"I hope I've got them all," Mom says, but I'm not really paying attention to her anymore. Kristen is setting the kitty in my arms.

And the kitty is purring. For me. She likes me. Her little, soft padded paws bat at my cheek. She begins to play with my hair.

"Look at that," Mom says in amazement.

The kitty snuggles her head between my neck and shoulder, settling in for a little rest.

"She looks cozy there, doesn't she?" Dad says.

"Can we name her that?" I ask. I want her to be cozy with me forever.

"Sure," Mom agrees. "That can be her everyday name."

"Everyday name?" Kristen asks. "What's that supposed to mean?"

"Well, according to T. S. Eliot—"

"Ugh," Kristen groans. Mom loves poetry, but Kristen can't stand it when Mom starts talking about her favorite poets.

Mom ignores Kristen. "According to T. S. Eliot, a cat needs three names. One's an everyday name, like Cozy. But then he says a cat needs a more dignified name. Something that allows it to keep its tail straight up and proud. Something so unique, no other cat in the world will have it. Cozycorium is a name I think Eliot would approve of."

The cat's purring vibrates against my chest. It almost feels like I'm purring, too. "But we can still call her Cozy for short, right?" I say.

"Right," Mom says.

"Wait," Dad says. "You mentioned three names. What's the third name?"

"Oh, well, Eliot says a cat will have a secret name that only it knows. It's a name that we'll never figure out. But whenever we see that she's deep in thought, she'll be thinking about her secret name."

"No," I say. "She's not allowed."

"Not allowed to what?" Dad asks.

"Have secrets from us. She can't have a third name."

Kristen laughs at me. "You can't stop her," she tells me. "Cats pretty much do what they want."

"I can too stop her," I insist. "I'm going to take her upstairs and show her my room now." I'm already halfway to the stairs.

"Madison," Mom calls after me, "what about all these be—"

IT SEEMS TO BE a pinecone. It has edges like one, and its round shape tapers toward the top the way pinecones do.

But I can't figure out how to make this thing work. The other items that have taken me places have been easy. I've tried imagining what it was like to hold them. To hand them to someone, to drop them, to put them on.

Something always works.

But not with this pinecone.

Maybe it's the Universe's idea of a joke. *Let's put this object with her that she can't quite figure out how to use*, it's thinking. *See how long it takes her to go crazy.*

Uh-huh. Not long. A person who's dead and conscious

and revisiting her life at every opportunity must already be crazy.

Still . . . it's almost as big a mystery as this whole how-did-I-even-die-anyway thing. How many different things can you do with a pinecone?

Maybe that's not even what it is.

beyond the boundaries
of any one life

age 17

Ohmygod, if I don't find that assignment *right* now, my English grade is going down the toilet!

I scurry frantically, pulling things out of my book bag for the third time this morning. I look everywhere. *Every-where.*

I glance at the clock. . . . Twenty minutes until Gabriel gets here to pick me up for school. I worked so hard on that paper, and now I can't find it. I did it last night at Gabe's house and emailed it to myself. I'll have to reprint it.

I switch on the computer quickly, and while I am waiting

for everything to boot up, I scramble to the bathroom for my toothbrush.

When I return, I log into my email account and open the message I sent from Gabe's house last night.

Ohmygod. Unbelievable. There's no attachment. How could I have sent an email to myself with the sole purpose of attaching that paper—then have forgotten to do it?

I grab my cell phone to call Gabe.

No answer.

My eyes smart as they fill with tears. Can I remember any of that paper? I'll have to try to rewrite it in fifteen minutes. I flip open my English textbook. There are the two poems by Emily Dickinson that I'm supposed to hand in an analysis of—first hour:

664

Of all the Souls that stand create—
I have elected—One—
When Sense from Spirit—files away—
And Subterfuge—is done—
When that which is—and that which was—
Apart—intrinsic—stand—
And this brief Tragedy of Flesh—
Is shifted—like a Sand—
When Figures show their royal Front—
And Mists—are carved away,

Behold the Atom—I preferred—
To all the lists of Clay!

1732
My Life closed twice before its close—
It yet remains to see
If Immortality unveil
A third event to me

So huge, so hopeless to conceive
As these that twice befell.
Parting is all we know of heaven,
And all we need of hell.

Reading these two poems this morning causes me to shiver in a way that I never have before, and I've read them, well, probably a hundred times. Perhaps I'm anticipating my own exit from this world into the next when my parents see my English grade—minus this one-hundred-point assignment.

No time to think about it now. Must write down whatever I can remember about my original paper.

My fingers fly over the keyboard, rattling away in a manic rhythm. Memories of words and phrases skitter through my mind. I wrestle them into sentences: "It is ironic that Emily Dickinson inquired of the journalist Higginson whether her poetry was 'alive' when the subject of so much of her poetry was death. . . . Her obsession with exploring the nature of individuality in the face of death demonstrates her belief in the power of the individual to transcend the boundaries of life itself. . . . Her poetic narrators face down a certain knowledge and understanding of their demise as they grapple, beyond the barrier of death itself, with a diminishing awareness of life. . . ."

What was that line about the "Tragedy of the Flesh" that I'd written? Something about how she believed something atomic lived beyond that tragedy? Wait . . . no, I closed the paper with that line, didn't I?

Ten minutes left. . . .

Hold on. I wrote something about how she isolated herself in life, her reclusiveness being a form of dress rehearsal for death itself, and its "partings" of hell. . . . How did I put that?

Words continue to patter their way onto the screen. Organization? What's that? No time to get these thoughts to build on one another.

Five minutes left. . . .

A sudden sense of déjà vu strikes me. It's like I've been through this moment in my life before, but . . .

Must just be the weirdness of trying to write about death.

Twice.

And about a poem with the line "My Life closed twice before its close"—I mean, who wouldn't be freaked out about that?

I ignore the sensation and go back to writing: "Dickinson's 'letter to the World / that never wrote to her' is a collection of poems that explore the depths of human emotion and its enduring ability to extend beyond the boundaries of any one life and into the experiences of humanity. Her body of work is the atom she left behind after 'this brief Tragedy of the Flesh.' That atom causes within readers a nuclear chain reaction of human connection."

Print . . . print . . . print. It's not printing fast enough.

Gabriel honks the horn at me. I swipe the papers out of the printer tray and then carefully open my folder. I *can't* lose this paper again. I will place it right here in the pocket where I *always* keep assignments that are due for . . .

I freeze. Then shiver.

There it is. The original paper.

Right. There. In. Front. Of. Me. Exactly. Where. It. Belongs.

It's staring at me with the all-seeing eye of Emily Dickinson.

How is this possible?

Gabriel honks again.

I'll take both papers and compare them in the car. I shiver once more as I pull the old paper from the folder—

I shouldn't have done it. And I know it the second I return to *Is.*

It seemed like such a small thing, letting myself find that original paper. Vanity, I know. The first version was so much better than the second. And, yeah, I wanted the better grade on it, but even more than that, I wanted my AP English teacher, Mrs. Bevery , to know how brilliant I was. I needed to hand in that first paper. I thought.

But now things are changing. A lot. More than they did when I messed with the whole handbag thing. That time it felt like the key in my song of life jumped up a half note. Now it seems like a whole different song is playing. Everything about space and time seems . . . different. And scariest of all . . . I'm forgetting who and what I was in the first version of life, the me who never found the original version of that Emily Dickinson paper. I'm afraid of losing her . . . *that* me.

It's like dying all over again. I'm going to the funeral of someone who I both hated and loved. And it's scary because I'm not sure if I'll be as happy with the me I just created as I was with the old one.

daddy-daughter dance

age 7

The music swirls around us. Sandra and I are both wearing the "spinningest" dresses we could find. We twirl around on the dance floor watching them spreading out in a circle around our hips.

Life couldn't be better. We're at the Daddy-Daughter Dance. There are colored lights all over the community-center gym. Our dads are both dressed up the way they usually are when they leave for work. But, right now, our dads belong just to us.

Daddy is holding both of my hands as we sway back and

forth to the music. Every once in a while, he winks at Sandra's dad and they both spin us around again.

Sandra and I giggle.

Next comes the "Hokey Pokey." I love this song. Daddy is so silly when he does the "turn yourself around" part. I'm laughing so hard, I have a sharp pain in my side. Sandra isn't laughing hard enough, so her dad tickles her.

For the next song, we change partners, and Daddy dances with Sandra. I dance with Sandra's father. Even though I like him, I notice he isn't as tall as my dad is. And he isn't as handsome, either.

Someday, I want to fall in love with a man like my daddy. Someone who makes me smile and giggle, someone who twirls me around, someone who knows how to have fun doing the Hokey Pokey.

When the end of the evening comes, I don't want to leave. I want to keep dancing, keep playing with Sandra. Tonight we're pretending to be sisters, and I don't want to ever stop.

But Daddy reminds me it's time to go, and he helps me put on my coat. I look in the pocket for my ticket. When we got here, I put it in my coat. I know I will always keep it. It's special. But . . .

The ticket isn't there.

I look again . . . still not there.

I start to cry. Daddy gets down next to me to ask what's

wrong. I tell him and tell him that my ticket is gone, but he keeps saying, "What? I can't understand you." I try telling him louder, but he still doesn't understand.

Sandra finally translates for me. "You lost your ticket?" he asks. When I nod, he pulls me into his arms and lets me sit on his thigh as he tries to dry my tears.

"We'll look," he promises. "Calm down so we can look."

Daddy, Sandra, her father, and I all look around the room . . . under tables, on the dance floor, on the chairs. The DJs are packing up all their musical equipment, and the janitors are starting to turn out the lights. The gym feels so lonely. All the magic is gone. Why couldn't it stay?

Daddy tells me we have to go now, even if we haven't found the ticket.

I cry harder. Daddy tries to comfort me by telling me that we can make a new ticket when we get home; that it'll be just as good as the real one, maybe even better. But he doesn't understand. I don't want to leave my ticket in this lonely place, all by itself.

Daddy promises me ice cream on the way home. But that idea doesn't make me feel any better. Mr. Simpson and Sandra finally leave. We look around the room one more time . . . no luck.

Daddy finally pulls me, still crying, from the room.

———

Back here in *Is*, I notice that the ticket is drab. It does not sparkle in pink and white the way I remember it. Instead, it just glows with a boring sameness.

Part of me wants to go back and allow my seven-year-old self to find it.

But I won't. No matter how hard she cries.

When I was alive, I thought I was always losing everything. But I wasn't. There are so few objects here in *Is* that can take me back to my life, I can't part with the ones I do have.

Lost, this piece of paper is my ticket back to the Daddy-Daughter Dance.

And it has to stay lost to keep me the person the night of the Daddy-Daughter Dance made me. . . .

Emily Dickinson referred to life as a "Tragedy of the Flesh." Losing that ticket was a tragedy to the seven-year-old me, but that tragedy shaped the soul "I have elected." Letting myself find that Dickinson English paper has already changed that soul some, but now I'm electing to feed and care for the one I have. I like it.

I swear Emily Dickinson's poetry makes sense to me in a way it never could have when I was alive.

gathering ghosts

I REMEMBER THIS HAIR CLIP. I remember when I lost it, too. . . .

age 13

We are (all ten of us) at my house. Somehow I've managed to convince my mother to allow us to have a slumber party here. We've been banished to the basement so our—as my mother condescendingly puts it—"girl giggle and gossip" won't disturb everyone else for the night.

And we are planning to make it through the whole night without sleeping.

So far, so good. We've watched three DVDs, eaten four bags of Doritos and three pizzas, and plowed through several two-liters of Coke (caffeine buzz, anyone?). And we're having a riot fainting. It's the coolest feeling I've ever had. Tammy taught us how to do it (don't ask me where she learned). First, we hyperventilate while bending over (gotta get all that blood to the head). Then we pull ourselves up quickly and Tammy presses in this one spot, right between the ribs, and—out we go.

The first time I did it, I fell backward onto the couch and lost my new hair clip. I love that hair clip, and I'm sure that it's somewhere under the couch or between the cushions, even though I can't find it. Still, even the loss of my favorite new hair clip isn't enough to discourage me from fainting a few more times.

Or maybe even seven more. It's such a great feeling. It's as if *everything* in the world disappears. It's like gliding on space for a few seconds. I feel both conscious and unconscious all at once, and wish I could stay that way. But eventually full consciousness seeps across the fabric of my mind, soaking everything in reality.

As I'm getting ready to faint the ninth time, Tammy says she doesn't want me to do this anymore. She thinks it might not be very healthy. Is *anything* fun *ever* healthy?

Still, she might have a point. I don't know why I suggest it, but since fainting appears to be coming to an end, I say,

"How about if we get out the Ouija board?"

Cindy groans. "C'mon, Maddy. It's two o'clock in the morning. Can you pick a creepier time to do that?"

Amber punches her in the arm. "That's the point, dummy."

"I think it sounds like fun," Sandra—ever the best friend—says. "Where is it?"

"I'll get it," I assure everyone. But I'm only halfway up the stairs before I get a major case of the creeps. I run back down. "I can't do it," I say. "It's too creepy up there."

Everyone laughs at me, but Sandra says, "I'll go get it for you. Tell me where to look."

"It's in the family room closet with all the other games."

Sandra glides up the stairs and disappears. A flash of jealousy streaks through me at the way her thin, graceful body seems to float up the stairs, her thick hair waving behind her. Not a single clunk or pound on the way up. Incredible. How does she do that gliding thing?

While Sandra's gone, the rest of us talk about who's going to go first and what questions we should ask the board. It takes Sandra longer than it should to come back, but she finally reappears. As she hands me the game, she says, "Sorry. I went to pull it out of the closet, and a few other games came with it. Made a bunch of noise. I had to pick the other games up, and your mom came downstairs and yelled at me."

I roll my eyes. I can tell we're both thinking the same thing. My mom yelling at Sandra doesn't even come close to the way Sandra's mom yells at me. But I don't say anything about that. Sandra's totally embarrassed by the way her mother treats me.

Amber and Lacey set up the board. They're going to go first, and they want—naturally—to ask for the answer to an important question plaguing the universe: Who is Amber going to go to prom with her senior year? D-O-U-G-P-R-E-S-T-O-N the planchette spells on the board. Amber is outraged. Doug Preston has wanted to hook up with her for almost a year now, and she's not interested.

"You pushed it," Amber accuses Lacey. "You wanted it to say that!"

"I swear I didn't," Lacey counters.

Everyone else is laughing. "It's not funny," Amber protests. "It's her turn to find out who she's going to prom with her senior year!" She puts a serious and mysterious look on her face and demands that the board tell her the answer to this question.

S-C-O-T-T-T-U-R-N-E-R the planchette spells. Scott Turner is a total dork. No one is ever going to go to senior prom with him.

"Now *you're* pushing it," Lacey says.

"Ha, ha. It's not so funny now, is it?"

"Okay, you two, let someone ask it a real question," Sandra demands.

Cindy and Diane sit at the board, and Cindy asks, in the spookiest voice she can come up with, "Is there a spirit in the room with us?"

The planchette creeps its way over to the word *yes*. A quarter of an inch from the word, Diane screams and removes her fingers. Cindy forces the planchette off the board. "Ohmygod," Diane says, "I swear I wasn't moving that thing."

"Me, either," Cindy agrees.

"There's really a spirit here in the room with us," Diane says.

"Whooooaaaahhh." Amber's sarcasm rolls out along with the ghostly sound she makes.

Diane glares at her. "I mean it. You try asking the room if there's a spirit here!"

"No, thanks." Amber laughs. "I had my turn, and I already know how it works!"

"Oh, I'll do it." I sigh.

"I'll help," Tammy offers. "Will you pick up that whatever-it's-called thingy?" she asks Cindy, nodding toward the planchette. "It's by your feet."

"I'm not touching that thing!"

"What*ever*," Tammy says, and leans over to grab it. "It's just a game, you guys."

She places the planchette back on the board and looks expectantly at me. "Who's asking the questions?" she wants to know.

"I'll do it," I offer. The other girls gather around us, and I ask, half joking, "Is there a spirit in the room?"

Tammy and I hold our hands steady, trying to relax to see if the planchette will move on its own.

It does.

Really.

I truly don't think Tammy's doing anything to it, because her face is turning ghostly white. "Stop it," she whispers to me.

"I'm not doing anything," I tell her honestly.

As the planchette spells out I-S-E-E-Y-O-U, the other girls become deathly quiet. All jokes have ended.

My fingers are shaking. I don't want to know the answer to my question, but I feel compelled to ask it anyway. "Who do you see?" Even my voice is shaking.

M-A-D-I-S-O-N.

It's my turn to glare at Tammy. "You're doing this, aren't you?"

"No. I swear. I'm not."

And I have to believe her, because her hands are shaking, too.

"Who are you?" I ask the room.

L-I-K-E-Y-O-U-I-A-M-D-E-A-D.

Cindy screams.

"*Shhh!*" I yell at her. "Shut up. You're not the one that's getting told you're dead, all right? So just shut up!"

"Why are you here?" Sandra asks the room.

Tammy stands up suddenly, knocking over the chair. Sandra takes her place at the table. "Put your fingers back on the planchette," Sandra tells me. I don't much want to—at this point, who would?—but I've taken orders from Sandra most of our lives.

I-A-M-S-O-R-R-Y.

Amber starts giggling. "Way to freak us out, Simpson. Could we be stupider? Why are we trying to scare ourselves to death?"

"*Shh,*" Diane tells her.

"Who are you?" Sandra asks the room again.

T-A-M-M-Y.

The room is silent for a second, and then Tammy yells, "This is a bunch of crap! You guys are making fun of me, aren't you? I'm outta here."

She storms up the stairs.

I jump up to follow her. "Wait! Tammy! I'm not doing it. Honestly."

She turns on the stairs and gives me a glare like nothing I've ever seen from anyone. In the last thirty seconds I have somehow become her enemy. "You can't go anywhere, Tammy," I say. "It's the middle of the night. You can't walk home right now."

"I'm leaving. I'll call my mother from upstairs. She'll come get me, even if it is the middle of the night. I'm not staying here with any of you guys. I hate you all."

She turns again and goes the rest of the way up the stairs. I run aft—

```
┌─────────┐
│   is    │
└─────────┘
```

GRIEF THROBS THROUGH ME.

Because this night is the end of my friendship with Tammy—at least as we knew it.

It's pretty weird the way all these trips back are helping me remember most of my life. I remember now how after that night with the Ouija board we all managed to convince ourselves that there weren't really any ghosts in the room. We got good at turning it into a joke.

But now I know there actually was a ghost in the room. Because I was there.

And now I know there was another ghost there, too.

Tammy.

There are things that bother me about this moment in my life. I return to it time and again to try to puzzle them out. I am careful every time I return to never look too hard for the hair clip. Returning to this moment provides me with the only true companionship I have in this new existence—the ghost of Tammy.

Ironic, huh? That night ended our friendship—at least our living one—but now it seems she's my only companion.

True, she's the only other *dead* person I've met. Apparently desperation makes the heart grow fonder.

I just wish she'd answer all the questions I have.

I want to ask her, how did you know I was there? I didn't realize you were until you revealed yourself. What did you lose that allowed you to return to that moment? How did you die? And *when* did you die?

There might be a lot of my life I still don't understand, but I have noticed that no item has ever taken me past the age of seventeen. That's also where all the memories I'm now having seem to end. Conclusion? It doesn't exactly require the deductive powers of Sherlock Holmes to figure out I probably died around then. And even though that idea freaks me out, another realization freaks me out even more. If I can travel to any moment in my previous existence where I lost an object, then Tammy can, too. That means she could have lived long after me. Reached the ripe old age of seventy-five. And then come back to that slumber party when we were thirteen just because she lost some stupid little object there.

It's a creepy thought. Disturbing. More than anything else in this afterlife has been.

There's another thing, too, that bothers me about this whole slumber party thing: Why—exactly—is Tammy's ghost apologizing to mine?

lost and found

age 16

It's a terrible habit, this need I have to hold something familiar whenever I'm nervous. I'm sliding into Gabriel's car on a warm spring afternoon. The sun has heated the car to a stifling, near-tropic temperature. Gabe's whirring the windows down and turning on the air-conditioning.

Taking my keys out? *Bad idea*, I tell myself. *Don't do it.*

But I do. I search my purse to find the keys to my house. Anxiety overwhelms me. New situation, new guy, first time in his car. What do we say to each other? Will this be anything like the short conversations we've had from time to time in the past two weeks? Courtesy of Sandra. After I turned down Gabe's invitation to a party, she told him that I was totally interested in him and that he just needed to give me a little time. So, every few days, he's been dropping by my locker between classes to chat.

Sandra thinks I ought to be on my knees thanking her, but I'm not feeling all that grateful to her at the moment. It's because of her that Gabe came to my locker today and asked if I wanted a ride home. And it's because I can't stand to be harassed by her anymore that I'm in his car. Well, that and the way I'm fascinated by Gabe's eyes when he looks at me. The green streaks flecking the blue seem to play hide-and-seek whenever the light changes.

I find my keys, pull them out of my purse, then clutch them firmly in my hand.

"I'll get it cooled off in here pretty quickly," Gabriel promises as he swivels one of the vents to blow straight at me.

Put those keys back, I tell myself. *Put them back in your purse right now before you lose them.*

Can he tell how hard I'm gripping them?

Gabe's fingers begin to tap out a rhythm in double time against the steering wheel. I'd take that for nerves, except I know it's not. He's a snare drummer in the band's drum line. Translating life into rhythm seems to be as much a part of Gabriel as breathing is for the rest of us mere mortals.

I recognize the cadence from football-season games. He deftly beats out a fight song as he battles the traffic getting out of the student parking lot.

Some guy driving a Honda Civic is taking too long to make a left-hand turn. When twelve feet of space opens up in the right-hand turn lane next to us, Gabe takes advantage of the split-second opportunity, swings into that lane, and makes a left from there. As the Honda honks at us, I say, "I didn't know you were so . . . determined."

He glances at me and smiles. "You should."

Yeah. I guess I actually do. He hasn't given up on me yet.

Then again, maybe he's just confident. When he showed up at my locker after school and said, "How about a ride home?" I must have taken a little too long to reply, because he pulled my jacket off the peg, handed it to me, and closed my locker. "C'mon," he said, and started off down the hall with the expectation I would follow. And I did. It was like I was attached to him by a string. He moved forward, I moved forward . . . all the way to his car.

Now he's talking about school—not exactly complaining (he doesn't really do that, I've noticed, about anything), but as close as he comes to it. He's talking about how much homework he has and whether he thinks he can manage to get it all done on time.

"You always somehow do," I remind him. "You have a perfect 4.0."

I, on the other hand, do not. My grades are not *too* bad: My GPA is a 3.5. But the only subject I have a perfect 4.0 in is English. I've always been in accelerated English. It's because words are just so much a part of me. I can't seem to separate them from who I am or what I think.

I've just never been very excited, though, by any other subjects in school, so I don't put a ton of effort into homework for them. As long as I'm getting at least Bs, I'm fine with that. I've never felt like I had to prove myself to anyone by getting perfect grades. Sandra, on the other hand, always has, so I can understand the mind-set. And I can tell Gabe has it.

"Okay," he says. "I know when I'm being told to shut up."

I look at him in surprise. Obviously, he doesn't.

"That's not what I'm saying," I tell him. "I'm just trying to reassure you that you'll get it all done."

He glances at me in surprise and then returns his eyes to the road. We come up to a stoplight, where he looks at me more carefully. "Sorry. I guess I'm just used to people being all . . . I don't know, competitive . . . about the grade thing, I mean."

I do know what he means. There's this little world in the upper echelons of the GPA ranking where everyone pretends to support one another, but actually they all see one another as a threat. Somehow, they think their A's mean less if other people earn them, too.

Not a game I play, but Sandra does. She feels like she has to make her mother's life easier by being the perfect child. I wonder who Gabe is trying to prove himself to.

"Hey," he says as the light turns green, "it's a beautiful day. Wanna go sit by the river for a little while before we go home?"

Alone?!

"Uh, sure," I say.

He grins at me and takes a right turn toward the park that sits along the banks of the Grand River.

It's a short drive, and we talk about memories we have of coming to this park back when we were kids.

He pulls into a parking space, switches off the engine, and takes his keys from the ignition. That's when I realize . . . I'm not holding *my* keys anymore.

He opens his door as if to get out of the car and then realizes that I'm looking frantically around me . . . seat, floor, area between the seat and the door. "What's wrong?" he asks.

"Um, I, well, I was holding the keys to my house when we got in the car, but I don't know what I did with them." I hold up my empty hands.

"You mean you'll be locked out of the house and at my mercy if we don't find them?"

"Well, actually, yes." I'm now dumping all the contents

of my purse onto the floor to see if I put the keys back in there without realizing it. *Wait*, I remind myself, *make sure you don't dump out the tampon, too*. Everything else is on the floor in front of me. No keys. I start throwing makeup, pens, and my wallet back into my purse.

When my purse is sitting back in my lap, Gabe says, "Here, let me look under the seat for you."

Suddenly his chest and shoulders are sprawled across my lap. I can feel his muscles moving as he shifts around on top of me, pulling my legs together, then moving them toward the driver's side. He maneuvers his body farther over mine, drops his head below the seat, and starts searching under it. His chest is warm and solid against my thighs, and I can't help wondering what it would feel like to have all of him lying on top of me this way, to . . .

He suddenly looks up and gives me this devilish grin that seems to ask, "Are we having fun yet?"

I can't help it. I smile. The urge to tease him back surges through me, and before I even have a chance to think about what I'm saying, out pops, "While you're down there, why don't you check and see if my underwear is there, too?"

Shocked, his head whips up so suddenly that it hits the glove box. "Ouch!" he says. He balances himself on his hand and then starts to scoot back across me until he can sit up. He stares at me expectantly, tapping his fingers on the steering wheel as I make him wait for the explanation.

"Seventh grade, remember? You and some of your friends dared Sandra and me to go skinny-dipping, and, while we were in the pool, you stole all our clothes."

He grins. "Yeah, I remember. But we gave them back."

"All except my underwear," I agree. "They've been missing ever since."

He laughs. "I swear I have no idea why they weren't with your clothes when we gave them back. And you think I've had them all this time? No wonder you're scared of me."

"Scared of you! I'm not scared of you."

"Terrified. You wouldn't even look at me when I came to your locker that first time."

"If I was a little uncomfortable around you, it wasn't because of my underwear. It had more to do with what you saw at the wedding."

He holds up his hands in a gesture of "Not my fault," then says, "I didn't see anything at the wedding. Honest." He tries to keep a straight face as he says it, but there's this mischievous quirk at the side of his mouth that gives him away. I give him an "Oh, yeah? Try again" look, and we both burst into laughter.

"Okay, so I saw something," he admits.

We laugh again, and then I say, "When did you decide you wanted to ask me out?"

"I plead the Fifth."

"Oh, come on," I say. "Just tell me."

A long moment of silence passes, but I figure I can wait him out. Finally, he kind of grins and says, "Oh, fine then. It was when we were walking up the aisle together. You tripped, and I had to sorta hold you up. That's when I thought, 'Hey, I wonder if this totally klutzy girl would go out with me.'"

"No way," I say, laughing.

"Well, okay, not exactly. But it was kinda cute, y'know? I mean, the way you grabbed my arm. Then when I looked down at you, I noticed your chest had all these intriguing freckles. Guess I thought it'd be pretty cool to go out with them, and maybe even with you, too. I mean, it's not like I had fun with you at the rehearsal dinner or anything," he teases.

"Ohmygod. I can see why you wanted to plead the Fifth. You and Dana had just broken up and you were probably on the rebound, looking for freckled chests to pass the time with."

"Um . . . no. I didn't want to answer the question because I thought you'd be embarrassed about tripping on the way up the aisle. You know, that plus the whole dress-and-barfing-later thing?"

Intelligent? Me? Not so much.

Still . . . the rebound issue is a valid point. And I remind him of that.

"Maddy," he tells me, "*I* broke up with Dana. She didn't

break up with me. I'd been thinking about it for a while anyhow. And the last fight just seemed like, you know . . . the end. I'm not on the rebound from Dana. For me, our breakup was a slam dunk. I knew exactly what I was doing when I broke up with her, and it was what I wanted."

This sounds great, but I'm still stuck on the fact that Gabe dated the same girl for *two years*. That's practically like being married. Gabe probably knows everything there is about having a relationship, and I know . . . nothing.

Gabriel shifts in the seat and says, "You know, there's a place we haven't looked for your keys yet."

"Where?"

"Right here." Suddenly Gabe's whole body is within inches of mine. He puts one arm on each side of me and reaches into the crack between the seat back and cushion, as if searching there for my keys . . .

But then we both seem to get distracted, and—who *cares* about keys?

He's kissing me.

And it's fantastic . . . The warmth of his lips against mine, the way our bodies are leaning into each other, the feel of his shoulder beneath my hand. I don't know how long this goes on, but eventually Gabe breaks the kiss. My lips suddenly feel lonely as he leans back. He holds up his left hand and dangles my keys in front of my face. "Had a feeling these would be back there," he says in a husky voice. There's an edge of triumph in it. Because of the keys? Or the kiss?

I don't care.

"C'mon," he says, and pulls away from me. Still holding my keys, he turns toward his open door, and just before I get my own door open, I hear him say, "No way."

I turn back toward him. "What?"

He has one foot out of the car, but now he's looking around, even digging in the crack behind his seat. "You won't believe this, but now I can't find *my* keys."

I burst out laughing. I've lived my whole life in the Land of People Who Misplace Items, and finally I have company there. I know I shouldn't take delight in Gabriel's predicament. . . . I should feel empathy, having just had the same experience myself. But instead, I'm satisfied to finally know I'm not the only idiot who can lose a set of keys from her hand in less than three minutes.

"It's not funny," he says, but he's also smiling.

I start helping him look for the keys . . . the floor on my side . . . the crack behind my seat (in case he lost his keys while looking for mine), under my seat . . .

"Aren't you going to look under *my* seat?" he asks.

I stare into his eyes for a moment. The quirk at the side of his mouth is back. A challenge.

What the heck? I think, and then I sprawl across his legs, reaching beneath his seat, my breasts pressed against his thighs.

"I don't see—" I start to say, but Gabe is gently turning me over so I'm lying across his lap. He brushes the hair away from my face, leans down, and kisses me again. Then he loosely wraps the ends of my hair around his wrist. I turn my face into his hand and kiss his palm, feeling against my lips the lines that track across it. I wonder if my name is etched somewhere on his lifeline.

I turn my head back to make eye contact with Gabe. He's smiling. He helps me sit back up. "No keys?" he asks.

"Not under there," I say. "At least, not the ones we're looking for right now."

We look some more for his keys, and he finally locates them on the ground just outside his open door. He holds both sets of keys up to show me that we've succeeded in our quest to find them.

"Ready to see the river?" Gabe asks, dropping my keys into my—

Back in *Is*, I feel startled—and stalked.

By death.

Gabriel is dead.

Like me.

That moment when Gabriel couldn't find his keys . . . at the time, I thought our affinity came from us both losing the same thing.

But that wasn't the only experience we were sharing.

The tugging, binding, magnetizing pull of that moment . . . I have only felt it one other time on my journeys back to haunt my own life. It was during that slumber party where a ghostly Tammy was hanging out.

My ghost and Gabriel's made some kind of spiritual contact, just as Tammy and I did at the slumber party. And the tragedy is that I didn't realize it at the time, while the ghostly me was reliving those moments in the car.

And I can't go back.

Neither can he.

We *both* found our keys.

A profound sense of loss is oddly accented by the presence of Gabe's companionship.

But I don't want his company now. Not like this. Not in death. Not as a ghost.

I want him to be alive.

I shouldn't be surprised to discover that Gabe is dead, too. I've sensed all along that he belonged here with me in *Is*. But somehow I've always imagined he was back on Earth, still living the life I knew him in.

I can't help grieving that I'll never return to that moment in the car . . . that moment when he first kissed me . . . that moment where I slid so gently from insecurity at being with him to the greatest sense of togetherness I'd ever had.

But I'm *glad* I can't, too. Those other moments that I've been re-returning to seem to fade a bit every time I go to them. It's kind of like reading the same book over and over. You keep trying to capture what you felt when you first read it, but the feelings just aren't ever as . . . magical.

I can't bear to have that happen to this experience with Gabe.

I guess I'm glad, too, that I can't go back to that moment and keep myself from finding these keys. What if I ended up ruining the moment of our first kiss?

Not being able to re-experience our first kiss is, in a way, heartbreaking, but to have never experienced that kiss at all . . . that would be self-breaking. I wouldn't even be me without that exact moment.

the underwear

age 12

Even though it's dark out, I feel completely exposed as I drop my underpants onto the ground. The water will be cold, but I don't care. At least when I'm in that pool I'll feel more covered up than I do standing here naked. Why was I stupid enough to play Truth or Dare in the first place? I was *sure* that if I chose "truth," Tammy was going to—horror of horrors—ask me if I had a crush on Gabe . . . and *he* was sitting right across from me. He and Roger had been biking down the road in front of Tammy's. They normally don't spend any time with us, but tonight they stopped. And pretty soon they were just hanging with us. Maybe they were bored, nothing else to do on a warm Saturday evening two weeks before the end of the school year.

But choosing "dare" was a mistake—definitely a mistake, I realize now, as I slip into the water as quickly and quietly as I can. It's freezing, *totally* freezing.

"They better not be watching," Sandra says.

Just exactly what I'm thinking.

"And you owe me for this," she adds.

No doubt about that. Not many friends would be willing to put themselves through this agony just so their BF wouldn't have to do it alone. I still can't quite fathom that Tammy has done this to me. "I dare you to go skinny-dipping in the neighbor's pool," she said just ten minutes ago. Hard to believe my whole life has changed in that time: I have become a girl who trespasses—naked—into someone else's pool.

Can I get arrested for this?

I think I'd rather not know.

We hear muffled laughter on the other side of the fence. Everyone is checking to make sure we're actually in the pool.

Humiliating. Thank God the pool lights are off. Thank God no one seems to be home.

The fence rattles.

"Ohmygod," Sandra breathes. "Someone's coming over."

First, Roger Myers appears over the top of the fence, then Gabe follows. More giggling on the other side. I'm about to scream in outrage, but Sandra smacks me on the head, "*Shh!* C'mon." She pushes off farther into the deep end to hide beneath the shadow of the diving board. I don't waste any time in following her.

Roger says, "We're just checking to make sure you're really skinny-dipping."

"Ohmygodohmygodohmygodohmygod," is the only thing coming out of my mouth.

"There's *no way* we're letting you check that out." Sandra obviously has more presence of mind than I do.

Roger laughs. "No choice. We'll just grab these"—he bends over and scoops up the pile of our clothing—"and check to make sure it's all there."

Carrying our clothes, he runs toward the fence. He throws them over (or tries to; Sandra's bra gets stuck on the top of the fence), then scrambles up after them. He rescues Sandra's bra and tosses it on the other side of the fence, then jumps down after it. Gabe shoots over the fence right after him.

"Oh. My. God." At least I've managed to change the tempo of my speech even if I haven't managed to find any new words.

"It's all here," Tammy announces, barely loud enough for us to hear. She doesn't want to get caught, either.

Roger's face reappears at the top of the fence. The

muffled giggling from below him is making me feel crazy. He tosses down our clothes. They rain into a scattered mess in the dirt; then Roger disappears again, and within seconds we can hear pounding feet receding into the distance as a giggling herd stampedes its way back to Tammy's.

Quiet hangs heavy in the air again. The only sounds we hear are the whorls our limbs make in the water.

"Time to get out," Sandra announces. We stumble over to our clothes. No towels, of course. Not one of the amenities offered to trespassers. The clothes stick to us as we put them back on.

"I can't find my underwear," I tell Sandra.

"Forget 'em," she says. "Let's just get *out* of here." Her long curly hair has already soaked the top half of her shirt. I can't help being satisfied with the messy look of it. Sandra's always dressed a bit too neatly. All her clothes—picked out by Mrs. Simpson, of course—are too well coordinated. Her socks, her hair clips, her shoes, everything all goes together. She sometimes looks like a present that's been professionally wrapped by someone who doesn't care at all about the gift inside the box. But as she stands here now, in a wrinkled and wet shirt, she seems more like the person I really know she is. "Hurry up," she prods me.

"I can't just leave behind my underwear," I protest.

"Sure you can," she insists. She grabs my arm and pulls me to the fence.

headache

age 16

The note comes back to me folded a few extra times.

Thank God. That must mean Sandra had an aspirin. My head is pounding.

Throbbing. In time to Ms. Winters's voice. Chemistry class. Just where a girl with a headache and major problems doesn't want to be.

I unfold the note carefully, and a yellow and red Tylenol Geltab rests on top of Sandra's writing. Right underneath my plea for an aspirin, she's written:

At least Winters is off on one of her tangents. You

won't have to know any of this stuff for a test. That must help with your headache.

I write back:

It would if she hadn't decided to get distracted by something so scientific and complicated. Every once in a while I actually try to get all this stuff to make sense. I liked it better the time we all managed to get her talking about her crazy brother for the entire hour. Whose idea was it to get her going on this quantum mechanics thing?

I pass the note back one seat to Sandra. We don't dare talk. We don't want to interrupt her in any way, or she'll remember that she's supposed to be teaching us about covalent bonds . . . that she's somehow gotten away from what she wrote in her lesson plans for today. Quantum mechanics isn't nearly as thrilling as some of the personal stories she tells us when her mind starts wandering, but it still means that in twenty minutes she'll realize we don't have any of the information we need to do our homework and— awesome—she won't give us any.

While I'm waiting for the note to come back, I contemplate trying to dry-swallow this Tylenol. I was hoping for an aspirin. They're smaller. This rubbery thing is likely to get stuck in my throat.

My day totally sucks.

The note comes back:

Uh . . . that would be your *boyfriend who started asking her how the rules of particle physics influenced the bonding of molecules. He was trying to get her off track, wasn't he?*

I take my time writing a response. Ms. Winters looks like she'll be going on and on for quite a while.

Probably. Are you following this whole thing she's trying to tell us about how subatomic particles can be both waves and particles at the same time? Those splatter pictures she's drawing make my head pound in pain. I want to throw a whole bottle of Tylenol through one of those slits and see if we get a particle or wave pattern, you know? And okay, so maybe it's amazing that something can be two things at once, and that observing them influences which of the two they are, but I'd rather set up a study to see how observation of that Web page influences Dana.

I pass the note back to Sandra. Ms. Winters has moved on to talking about how everything in the universe is connected in ways that can't always be seen or understood. This has something to do with photons behaving like both particles and waves. She calls this the particle-wave duality and wants to impress on us its importance: that at the subatomic level no time has to pass for one particle to know about and be affected by what's happening to another. At the smallest levels of the universe, rules of cause and effect become blurred because particles can communicate with one another simultaneously.

This is enough to make my brain explode, so instead of trying to make sense of it, I begin wondering what kind of interaction two subatomic particles would want to have, anyway. Might make an interesting short story for English class. Maybe I can give it a bit of an Edgar Allan Poe flair. One particle nukes another and then tries to hide its energy under a floorboard—or maybe in a wormhole. Thus, the second particle can never be observed again and have imposed upon it human expectations about whether it is a wave or particle . . . and therefore it can be *neither* particle nor wave . . . or maybe it would still then be both . . . but the universe's communication about the nuking event is simultaneous, so does that mean that the universe (and the humans trying to watch this event) have already taken into account—at the very moment it's happening—the event itself? Now, that would seem to take all the suspense out of the story. I mean, that's sort of like everything is predetermined, right?

Ohmygod. I can't escape subatomic thoughts. I'm definitely losing it. If I don't stop, my head isn't just going to explode, it's going to create nuclear fallout.

Thankfully, the note comes back.

You don't need to set up a study to find that out. She had a screaming and crying fit in the bathroom and everyone's talking about it.

Yeah. Everyone.

Except—apparently—me, since I've missed out on all the good gossip. That's what I get for hanging with Gabriel between classes.

Someone anonymously published on the Web a list of spiteful awards for Overton High School girls. Things like Most Emo, Aberzombie of the Year, and Biggest Babbler. Dana won in the Best-Looking Bitch category. I can't help feeling satisfaction that someone else has finally discovered the perfect description of Dana—even though I know that makes me a terrible person. Whoever published those awards really shouldn't have done it. That was way out of line. The author is entitled to his or her opinions (especially when they're so close to the truth), but putting that out there on the internet? Way unethical.

Still . . .

Missed all that. Details please.

A few minutes later, the note returns.

She was all crying in the bathroom because who would do something that terrible to her? She's never meant to hurt anyone, etc. Guess she was some bizarre combination of totally hurt and so angry she wanted to kill someone. Lacey was in the bathroom at the time, and it was enough to even make her feel sorry for Dana. Maybe this will be a turning point for her, and she'll start being nicer. Did you hear that Mr. Patterson already got the website taken down?

Is Gabe really worth this? First he earns me Dana's eternal enmity . . . then he keeps me from hearing all the good gossip when she's finally managing to get what she deserves.

I pass the note back:

How'd he manage to do that? I thought he didn't even know who did it.

It returns:

He called the people who host the Web page, and they agreed to take it off. Oh, and he's found out who did it. Lucky it wasn't you.

What the . . . ? *What do you mean?*

Dana was telling everyone that you were the one who must have made the page.

Me?! Oh, crap. The bells rings. I've got to take that Tylenol.

Where is it?!

felicity's shoe

"*Rrrghghgh!*" Cozy's claw slices across my wrist.

"Ouch!" I yell.

Perhaps the hat *isn't* such a good idea. Even as I think it, I continue trying to tie the ribbon beneath Cozy's chin.

"If you'd just hold still," I say through gritted teeth, "I'd have you all dressed."

Felicity, my American Girl doll, lies on the bed next to me, naked except for her tights. It seems impossible to get the tights on Cozy, so I haven't even tried, but Felicity's blue and white summer outfit looks very cute on the cat. An

American Girl pet: perfect. Just what I've always wanted—well, at least ever since the idea occurred to me ten minutes ago. But the cat won't cooperate with me. She struggles against me and uses her paw to try to push the beautiful straw hat off her head. The shoe I've worked so hard to put on her back paw goes flying through the air as she keeps struggling.

"Stop it," I tell her.

She caterwauls in response—loud enough for Kristen to hear. Now she's pounding on my door. "Maddy, *what* are you doing to that cat?" she demands. "Let me in."

Mom should know better than to leave Kristen as my babysitter. We fight *all* the time when she's babysitting for me. She won't let me have *any* fun.

Cozy's still yowling, and Kristen's still demanding to be let into the room. I try to hold the cat still as I crack the door open. Kristen pushes her way through, and I slam the door before Cozy can jump from my arms.

"What's going on?" Kristen asks. She stares in amazement at Cozy. I think the cat looks great dressed in 1780s clothing, but I can tell from Kristen's expression that she doesn't. "You're going to *ruin* your doll clothes," Kristen informs me.

"Will not," I say, even though I can see perfectly well that Kristen's right. The pretty blue hat ribbon I've tried to tie below Cozy's chin is in her mouth, and the sides of it are getting all icky.

Kristen tries to grab the cat away from me, and now we're playing tug-of-war with her. She yowls and scratches Kristen on the cheek. Kristen screams and lets go of Cozy. The cat slips from my hands, too. She somersaults end over end and lands squarely on all four feet. Kristen opens the door to let her out, and Cozy stumbles and trips over the Felicity dress as she races through the door.

"You did that just to be mean!" I yell. Kristen's *always* ruining anything I think is fun. Already today she's denied me an ice-cream cone, refused to let me swim at the neighbor's house, told me I couldn't watch TV because *she* wanted to watch it, and now this?!

Kristen snorts. "Oh, stop being such a baby."

"I'm not a baby."

"You are, too. If you don't get exactly your own way, you whine and cry. 'It's no fair,'" she mocks. "That's all you know how to say."

"Well you stink as a babysitter," I tell her. "I hate you. I'm going to tell Mom on you when she gets home."

Kristen laughs. "Go right ahead. Tell her how I spoiled all your fun torturing the cat. She'll give you a big lecture about why the cat hates you and runs away whenever she sees you coming."

"She doesn't hate me!" I yell louder, enraged. Kristen spins around and leaves my room. "But *I* hate *you*! I hate you, hate you, *hate* you!" I scream after her. When she still ignores me, I charge from the room, yelling, "Everyone hates you. You'll make a terrible mother! Your own kids will hate you. You're—"

```
┌─────────┐
│   is    │
└─────────┘
```

STILL TRYING TO figure out this pinecone thing . . . I try imagining that I'm putting it on a Christmas tree.

Nothing. I used to paint them for Christmas. I try imagining I'm doing that. But I'm still here in *Is*.

Mom used to spray them with cinnamon scent during the holidays and set them out in baskets around the house. There's no smell to this insubstantial ghostly pinecone, but I imagine myself back in a body, back in a place where smell is possible. And I try to imagine the smell of cinnamon and pine. I even imagine myself holding the cone close to my nose.

And I'm still here.

Maybe I played toss with it when I was a kid. I imagine throwing it back and forth with Kristen. With Sandra.
With Tammy.

Still here.

a penny for your thoughts

age 17

"I think I have enough money," I say, digging around inside my wallet to check. I'm even counting pennies. I really want to buy these Robeez baby shoes. They are the cutest thing ever.

Too much in my hands . . . shoes, change, wallet, purse. I drop my wallet on the floor, and change scatters everywhere.

"Don't you dare!" I tell Kristen just as she and her eight-months-pregnant belly are about to bend over and help me. "Here, hold these instead," I say, handing her the baby shoes and my purse. I get down on my hands and knees and start crawling around on the floor, scrounging up my change.

Kristen laughs at me. "You look pretty funny," she says.

"Yeah, well, so do you," I tell her, but not unkindly.

She grins down at me. "The pregnant body is a beautiful body."

From down here her stomach looks even bigger. It's a wonder she doesn't just explode. "That from one of your pregnancy books?" I ask.

"Yeah," she admits. "I'm trying hard to believe it. Supposedly, I can have my real body back someday. Hard to imagine, though."

It is. But I don't tell her that. I have most of the change. I can see a penny under the rack, but there's a dust bunny with it, and I'm *not* touching *that*. I'm wealthy enough to suck up a one-cent loss.

"Just remember—" Kristen starts to say as I stand up.

I've heard this so often I can finish the sentence for her. "Take extra precautions when you're on an antibiotic."

Kristen wasn't planning on becoming a mother at twenty-four with only a year and a half of marriage behind her. She had been taking the pill, but then she had to take antibiotics to fight an infection. Apparently, they reduce the effectiveness of the pill, so . . . whammo, she was pregnant. She's paranoid that the same thing will happen to me.

Not that she needs to be.

Gabe and I aren't doing anything that would get me pregnant. Don't get me wrong. I think we've tried *everything* else there is to try. We're having . . . well, a lot of fun. So much fun, it doesn't seem like we're missing out on all that much. Besides, just about the time we were thinking about the whole sex thing, Kristen got pregnant.

All in all, watching your older sister puking every day is a pretty effective form of birth control. One time when she was at our house, she vomited so violently that she slammed her head against the toilet seat and had a giant bruise on her forehead for, like, a week and a half. And those first three months, it seemed like she was in bed with a headache whenever she was lucky (?) enough not to be feeling nauseated.

"If you and Gabriel are—" Kristen begins. I know this offer, too: She's willing to take me to the doctor, to help make sure Mom doesn't know, yadda, yadda, yadda. . . .

"We're not," I say. Then, to change the subject, I pull an adorable green baby outfit off the rack. "Isn't this cute?" It's mint-colored and has a doggie and a kitty playing together on it.

"Since when do dogs and cats play together?" Kristen asks.

I roll my eyes. "C'mon. Children's clothes teach an important lesson. This outfit is trying to tell the baby that everyone can get along together if they just try."

I admire a pretty pink outfit on the next rack over. It has beautiful combinations of pink and orange and yellow flowing together in a floral print. "I love this one," I tell Kristen. "Too bad we don't know whether you're having a girl or a boy."

In this day and age, who doesn't know that before the baby's born? I just don't get why Kristen doesn't want to know what sex her baby is. I'm reduced to having to find every possible cute outfit in green—the only color they make unisex baby clothing in. Well, okay, that's not exactly true. There are a few yellow outfits that can go either way, too. But it seems like they all have ducks on them, and how many ducky outfits can a kid stand?

"What's the point in knowing?" Kristen asks. We've had this conversation before, so we both approach it a little wearily.

"Uh . . . let's see . . . planning the baby's room, buying clothes ahead of time, just knowing what to expect when you bring the baby home."

"Madison, it's not as if I'd know the baby any better just by knowing it was a girl or a boy. I'm going to have to get to know it after it's born anyway. Knowing the sex of the kid wouldn't really help me know who the kid's going to be. Sometimes I'll be driving along, and I'll wonder what this person inside me is going to turn out like, you know?

I'll be thinking about the kid riding around in the car seat and wondering if it's going to fall asleep back there because it likes the car. Or maybe it'll hate the car and cry. I wonder what the kid's going to laugh about for the first time. And none of that seems to have anything to do with whether the kid's a boy or a girl."

"Yeah," I say, "but if we knew you were having a girl, I could buy her this way cute outfit."

"Get off it, already," Kristen says. "There are far more amazing things to wonder about than whether the baby will be a boy or a girl."

"Like what?" I ask.

"Like, that this person has never been alive before. There was a time when he or she didn't exist. And now this kid *does* exist. So much of its destiny is already being determined from inside of me. How can that be? I mean, where really does life come from?"

"Uh . . . too philosophical for me?"

"Doesn't it just blow you away? That someone can *not* exist and then all of a sudden *exist*? Where was this person before conception?"

"Is this another side effect of pregnancy?" I ask.

"What?"

"All this wondering about life, the universe, and everything in it?"

"Maybe. I don't know. Some women start cleaning their

houses frantically. Not me. I still can't stand cleaning. But I guess I do have some bizarre and deep need to understand *life* now that there's another life inside me."

We're quiet for a moment, both looking at outfits. There's another green one that's a possibility. I pull it out and show it to Kristen. She suddenly asks, "Do you think I'll make a good mom? You know, a lot of this kid's life has already been determined. But there are some things that I can still influence. Wonder if I'll do it right."

Okay, I could come up with some kind of smart-ass remark worthy of the younger sister.

In fact, it's tempting.

But there's something so serious in her expression, so insecure, so at the whim of fate, that I can't do it. "Of course you'll make a great mother," I tell her.

"I don't know."

"I do. I've been the understudy for the part of your child several times. I know what I'm talking about."

"You're biased."

"True. But you have to remember that even if there's no one else in the world who loves you as much as I do, there's also no one else who can possibly hate you as much as I've hated you over the years. That makes me qualified to assess the situation."

Kristen smiles at me. "Thanks, Maddy. Let's get the green outfit. If you don't have enough money to pay for the baby shoes, I'll get them. They *are* cute."

"I want to get them," I protest. "I'm sure I have enough money. Wouldn't it be great, though, if I could convince Mom and Dad to get me a credit card?"

"No way. I *know* what you'd spend your money on."

We start walking toward the registers. "Oh, come on . . . I'm not that bad. And then I'd have the money to come back and buy that cute little pink outfit in another month if you end up having a gi—"

is

A NEW QUESTION EMERGES: Did my sister give birth to a boy or a girl?

I'm convinced I would remember whether her child was a boy or a girl, convinced I'd even remember its name—if I ever *knew*. After all, so many other things have come back to me through these visits home, and Kristen's baby is so fundamentally a part of her that I *know* I would remember this baby if I'd ever met . . . him? Her?

So what this means is . . .

I must have died before the baby was born.

Kristen was eight months pregnant, so I must have died some time in the month following that trip to the store.

Without ever becoming an aunt.

I think of all the great mysteries that humankind has made progress toward resolving: the Big Bang, human evolution, weather prediction, the whole Einstein relativity thing.

The one little mystery I want resolved seems so small by comparison. I just want to know who my sister's child is. I want to know about one little person in the whole history of the world. Why can't I?

Okay, so maybe that's not such a "little" mystery after all. I mean, maybe that's the entire mystery of life—who we are, why we exist.

Still, I feel cheated. My life was interrupted right in the middle of an important plot element.

Back when I was alive, whenever I read ghost stories, the ghost always haunted other people. It went into the future to see what was happening in the world as life went on for the living. It got to find out what happened to the other characters in its story.

I can see why living people would dream up that vision of ghosts. No one wants to believe life ends this way . . . interrupted, unresolved, and unfinished.

Now that I'm a ghost I know the truth: Not only is my life incomplete, but I'm imprisoned by it, too. I never get to see beyond the boundaries of what I have already experienced.

I think back to Kristen's musings about the nature of

existence . . . and nonexistence. Her wonder about who and what her baby was *before* it was conceived. Now I wonder the same thing. Who was *I* before I existed? Who am I now that I no longer *do*?

It strikes me that this death thing is a lot like being in utero. My niece or nephew was alive inside my sister when she was eight months pregnant, but that baby didn't have the freedom to set any of the boundaries of its existence. It was locked into a dark place.

Just like I am now.

And before the pregnancy? Where was that baby then? Did it exist . . . at all?

Maybe that's the next stage in my trip. . . . I'm going to arrive at being nothing at all. . . . Death might just be the opposite of pregnancy . . . going through this dormant stage before arriving back to where we started . . . nonexistence.

Where is God?

When I was alive, I wasn't very religious. I mean, I didn't go to church and stuff like that, but I believed there was a God.

Now I wonder if there is. I sure want one. I want more than this . . . nothing. I want to feel like more than just some subatomic . . . thing . . . that can't decide whether it's a wave or a particle so it's both. Only in my case I can't seem to decide whether I'm alive or dead.

I'm both.

rattled

"Eeeeee eeeee eeeeeee eeeee eeeeeee eeeee eeeee eeeee eeeeeee eeeee eeeeee eeeeee!"

Sh-ch-sh-ch-sh-ch. Sh-ch-sh-ch-sh-ch. Ch-ch-sh-ch-sh-ch-ch.
SH-CHRACK!

"Aaaahhhhh! Aaahhhh! Ahhhhh! Ahhhhh!"

"Shshshsh! Shshshsh . . . Shshshsh . . . Hhhhmmmm . . . mmmmmm . . . mmmmmm . . . hhhhhhh . . ."

Okay. That one was . . . creepy.

My journeys back to life have been mysterious before this, but when I've returned I've always I understood what happened. I've remembered the events I experienced. But this time it is as if I experienced nothing.

No, that isn't right. I have a memory of definitely experiencing something, but it is . . . so difficult to put into words.

Color, warmth . . . the sounds of crying and humming. A voice and a smell and a touch I know well. My mom's.

She's the rock and the foundation of this experience.

But what happened in that scene? I must have lost my rattle. It's the object that returned me to life. Did I cry? Did my mother pick me up? Comfort me? Soothe me? The rattle is still here, so she must not have been able to find it for me.

I'm disconcerted by the whole experience and its myriad mysteries, afraid of being sucked into that black hole by gravity, of becoming that baby who has no words to express the impressions of her mind.

There's no way I'm going anywhere near that rattle again.

cell communication

The door opens. I step across the threshold and announce the obvious into my cell phone: "I'm here."

"So I see," Gabe replies, tapping END on his cell. I do the same, noticing a strange scent in the house. I can't quite identify what it is.

He doesn't exactly look thrilled to see me. Uh-oh.

We had plans to go out, but Gabe called me a half hour ago and said, "Sorry, I just can't go tonight." I asked what was up. His voice sounded odd, sort of quavery and distant, but he wouldn't tell me what was wrong. Just said again that he couldn't go, was really sorry, would call me tomorrow.

Too strange.

I just didn't feel right letting it go. I was worried about him.

So that's when I made the (possibly bad) decision to come visit. And I did at least warn him I was coming. (Oh, okay, so I didn't give him a whole lot of warning about that. But calling him as I was walking up his driveway was better than nothing, right?)

Now that I see the frown on his face, I'm thinking maybe that wasn't so much better than nothing. He's wearing a what-are-you-doing-here expression. This deflates me. I'm used to the you-light-up-my-life one (even if that's corny, it's true) that usually crosses his face every time I approach.

My stomach takes a dive down to my toes. What if . . . ? How can it have taken me so long to figure out that he might have ditched me for some other girl?

Maybe even Dana.

Is she . . . *here*?

My expression must reveal my absolute horror as I ask, "Is there some other girl?" because appalled shock flitters in his eyes as he says, "Is *that* what you think?"

"Well . . . I didn't. But it suddenly occurred to me just now."

He sighs. "Maddy . . . no. No way in hell." He steps

forward and puts his arms around me. "That's not it at all. I'm just . . . in a bad mood. I couldn't be decent to anyone tonight." He pulls away as suddenly as he enfolded me.

Strange again.

"But why?" I'm pushing it here, and I know it.

"I don't want to talk about it."

"Okay. I'm sorry. I'll just leave." I turn to go, hoping he'll stop me, but instead he opens the door to help me on my way. I'm contemplating how appropriate that saying is about not letting the door hit you on the way out when there's a crashing sound upstairs. It's followed by the ceiling shuddering in protest from whatever's happening on the floor above. Gabe's dad.

And suddenly everything makes sense.

Horrible sense.

Ohmygod, I recognize the smell that's been bothering me since I arrived. How could I have been so idiotic? I'm dense.

Now Mr. Archer is stumbling down the stairs. I want to flee the house, spare Gabe the embarrassment. But I can't seem to move.

The smell of alcohol gets stronger as Gabe's father descends. He appears at the bottom of the stairs, bloodshot eyes trying to focus on me. I nearly choke in the cloud of alcohol surrounding us all now.

"Is this the new girlfriend, Gabe?" he asks.

I glance at Gabe, but he won't even meet my eyes. "Yeah, I am," I say. He's never officially called me that, so amid all this other discomfort I start to wonder if I'm being presumptuous. Can this situation get any more nightmarish?

Uh . . . yeah. It can.

"Invite her to stay, Gabe," he says. He tries to slap Gabe on the back but stumbles into him instead.

Gabe still won't meet my eyes. I can tell he wants me as far away from here as possible, and, okay, let's be honest, I feel like he's shutting me out.

It hurts.

But so does the pain emanating from Gabe, and more than anything, I want to make Gabe's life easier.

"Uh, sorry," I say. "I can't stay. My mom's expecting me home."

Gabe's dad grins. At least I think that's what he's doing. Hard to tell in his current state.

"Well, then, I'll leave you two to say good-bye to each other." Now he's trying to give us some kind of I-know-how-you'll-say-good-bye-to-each-other look. Disgusting. It would be horrific on any parent, but a drunk one? "I just came down to get . . ." Mr. Archer gets lost in his thoughts.

Then he suddenly remembers why he made the Great Trek down the stairs. "Crackers. I want some crackers. I'll get those and go back upstairs." He toddles his way to the kitchen.

"Call me tomorrow?" I ask. I'm terrified Gabe will never talk to me again now that I've intruded into this grim scene from his life.

He doesn't say anything.

I swallow hard. "Is there anything I can, y'know, do for you?"

Gabe finally meets my eyes, reaches for my hand, and says, "Yeah."

I wait. And wait.

"What is it?" I finally ask.

"Stay," he says.

"I thought . . ."

He puts a finger to my lips to stop me. "I know," he says. "And you were right. I did want you to leave. But now I want you to stay."

He leads me into the living room and we sit on the sofa. He puts his arm around my shoulder, and I lean into him. "Why'd you change your mind?" I ask.

"You've already seen the worst."

"I'm sorry. I shouldn't have just marched over here. It was just, well, you didn't sound so hot on the phone, and I thought something was wrong, and, well, it was, but still I should have respected your need for privacy because I should have known you wouldn't just dump me for the night without some reason, and that you'd tell me if you wanted me to know, and—"

"Take a breath," Gabe interrupts.

"Huh?"

He squeezes my hand. "Take a breath. Calm down. It's not the end of the world. I'm fine. We're fine. And now you know."

"But I don't."

He looks at me quizzically.

"I don't know at all. What it's like, I mean. To deal with all this. To be you."

We hear his father stumbling up the stairs.

Gabe sighs. "It's been a year since the last time he had anything to drink. Then tonight—wham! Well . . . not even tonight. I came home this afternoon and he was already blotto. Must've come home from work early. Who knows how much he managed to drink before I got here? I tried to throw away what alcohol I could find, but shit—"

Okay, *this* surprises me. Gabe doesn't swear. At least not around me. This draws my attention to how worked up he is.

"—when he gets like this he hides that fucking stuff who-knows-where."

Now I'm getting freaked. The *F* word?

"The thing is," Gabe goes on, "I somehow feel like I can keep him from drinking so much if I stay here with him."

My heart quivers as I come to understand *why* it always feels to me as if Gabe is . . . *older* than me. "Gabe, I don't know anything about alcoholism, but I do know that I've never been able to keep my parents from doing something they were determined to do. Can you actually *stop* your dad from drinking?"

He sighs again, pulls away from me, and flops over sideways on the sofa. "I don't know," he says. At least I think that's what he's saying. It's hard to tell for sure because he's mashed a pillow on top of his face.

I try to pull the pillow away from him, but he's strong.

"The thing is," he says, "I know he manages to drink even when I am here. But how much *more* would he drink if I weren't here to try to stop him?"

Obviously not a question I can answer.

"Maybe having to try to hide what he's doing from me slows him down some, y'know? Then again, maybe I'm just fooling myself thinking I'm doing any good at all."

I'm still scrambling around in my head trying to find a reply to this when he says, "Still, if there's a chance I'm making it better, I have to try."

Seems like a psychologist would have a few things to say about that. But even if *I* could figure out that he was taking on too much responsibility here, it doesn't seem like *he's* quite ready to think about that.

I run my fingers through his hair. I'm not sure exactly what I'm managing to say with that, but it seems to work. He lets me pull the pillow farther away. I stretch out next to him and navigate my way between his face and the pillow.

And since we're horizontal anyway . . .

And since his dad has disappeared into an upstairs stupor . . .

And since the feel of Gabe's lips on mine and his hands wrapping around my waist is so fantastic . . .

Yeah. Well . . .

At least until Gabe's dad stumbles back down the stairs. We sit up quickly as he wanders into the living room. Mr. Archer looks at me all surprised. And even though I know he's drunk, it's still a little disconcerting to be so easily forgotten. Makes me wonder what other important things about his son he forgets when he's like this.

Then Mr. Archer wanders into the kitchen, and things start clattering out there. Gabe jumps up and starts taking care of Drunk Daddy Dear, so I tell him, "I better go. I told my mom I wouldn't be gone long."

"I'll call you tomorrow," Gabe promises.

I decide I should call my mother to tell her I'm on the way home. That's when I realize I don't know where my cell phone is because—and this is totally me—I set it down somewhere when I came in and wasn't paying any attention to what I was doing. We check every surface in the living room and the front entry hall. We look under the sofa. Behind the cushions (no kissing detours there this time, unfortunately). In desperation, Gabe finally uses his cell phone to call mine. We track the sounds of Beethoven's "Für Elise" back into the entryway.

Where my purse is sitting on the entryway table.

Imagine that. For once, I put something where it belongs.

No wonder I couldn't find it, I think in disgust as I open the bag to pull out—

infected

They're my favorite pair of earrings . . . made from old watch parts. No one else I know has a pair like them. But one of my ears has become so infected that turning my head hurts, so I take the earrings out. I wish I had a convenient pocket to put them in.

The doctor pulls the bandage away from the ulcer on Mrs. Simpson's calf. The sight of it . . .

My earring makes an unscheduled landing on the white-gray tile of the exam room floor, and the contents of my stomach are about to proceed to the nearest exit.

A few minutes ago, the doctor said, "You girls should give us some privacy." Now I understand *why*. One patient is enough. Cleaning up after us won't exactly make anyone's day around here.

But here we are anyway because Mrs. Simpson's reply to the doctor was, "My daughter can stay. Can't you, Sandra?"

So we stayed.

Unfortunately.

I swallow extra hard—several times—hoping to keep all previously ingested substances proceeding in an orderly fashion on their journey through the digestive track.

Why did Sandra's mom encourage us to stay?

I glance at Sandra. She looks . . . stressed. No . . . *distressed* would be a better word. She wants to take her mother's pain away. A powerful force of will emanates from Sandra's eyes, an unexpected strength at odds with the soft green of her irises. She believes she can heal her mother through will-power.

I'm pretty sure she *can't*. That would bring the force of Sandra's will up against her mother's. And Mrs. Simpson doesn't intend to get better.

That sounds cynical, I know, but I think it's true. Having an ulcer that mysteriously *won't* heal no matter what the doctors do . . . returning to the doctor's office every week . . . all the attention . . . yeah, this is so Mrs. Simpson's thing. She definitely gets off on it. Apparently, the ulcer's been bad for a while now, but in the last few days, infection has set in . . . wonder how *that* happened. Has she been doing any of the things the doctors have told her will help? Or is she hoping this ulcer will become bad enough that she'll need that skin-graft surgery she keeps mentioning? And, gee, won't that just be *such* a risk to her life? To hear Mrs. Simpson talk about it, you'd think it would be. I'm sure she'll need the entire universe to revolve around her for a good year after that.

And Sandra doesn't see how badly her mother *wants* to be sick.

So there she is, all sympathy, trying to will away her mother's ulcer, and I'm the only one her force of will is working on. My eyes are magnetically drawn to the same location Sandra's are gazing—the ulcer.

It's as large as my fist. It's mostly raw and bloody-looking—except for where the infection has started to set in. That's whitish, and it's oozing pus.

Suppurating.

I remember reading that word once in a book about a wounded Civil War soldier. I wondered at the time who in their right mind would ever use that word.

I glance up at Mrs. Simpson's face and see an expression that terrifies me . . . the pure joy on her face is evil. She's *glad* to see Sandra suffering for her.

And the word *suppurating* flashes in my mind again. It's the perfect word to describe this thing on Mrs. Simpson's leg.

And the perfect word to describe her soul.

"I'll be in the waiting room," I tell Sandra, then stomp out of the exam room.

The earring I dropped just doesn't matter anymore.

the spoon

age 17

Ben and Jerry's Cherry Garcia . . .

The best ice cream in the world.

But I still can't eat it. There's a walnut stuck in my throat. I can't swallow around it, and yet I won't allow myself to cry because Kristen's trying so hard to make me feel better. I stab at the ice cream with a teaspoon, making little half-moon indentations in it.

"C'mon, Maddy," Kristen says. "I'm sure it's going to be okay."

Yeah. No matter how this turns out, her life won't

change at all. It'll be just fine for her. Me? Oh, crap. That walnut in my throat just got even bigger.

I can't stand the sight of the ice cream anymore. Besides, the whole world-around-me-getting-blurry thing is making me feel more and more like crying, so I set the ice cream down on the picnic table behind me. "Don't let me forget to take that home," I manage to choke out of my tight throat. Thank God for something mundane I can talk about. That makes it a little easier to elude the tears trying to escape. "Mom will kill me if I leave that spoon here." As Kristen and I were leaving for the park, pints of ice cream in hand, there was Mom trailing along like a magnet attached to the spoons, warning us, "We're getting low on teaspoons. Don't you dare lose those. I mean it. Wait! I'll get you plastic spoons instead."

We were so out of there before she could get back with the stupid plastic spoons.

"Oh, screw Mom," Kristen says. It comes out in this completely offhand way, like she's announcing that Mom will be home from work on time today. It cracks me up.

But the laughter that wants to escape seems trapped behind the tears, and suddenly it's *all* gurgling up to the surface. Tears, sobs, laughter.

Oh, gross! It's just way too much for my body, and now there's snot trying to explode from my nose.

Kristen to the rescue with a fast move for the napkin.

She holds it out to me, and I blow my nose. Well, kind of. Kristen's trying to hug me, so the blowing thing's not working too well. I've never really known before how important balance is to successfully blowing the nose.

"Everything will be fine. I'm sure it's just your imagination."

Gee, so much for comforting me, Big Sis. Telling me I imagined all this? When I saw with my very own perfectly functional eyes that Gabe was walking along with his arm around Dana's shoulders? Now *there's* a way to totally infuriate me. "I saw them, Kristen, and it was *not* my imagination. They were walking along together and he had his *arm* around her *shoulders*. There's no mistaking that. Or what it means."

"Yes, there is, Maddy. You've always been especially good at taking what's right in front of you and drawing the wrong conclusion from it. Remember that pregnant woman at the store when you were little?"

Way unfair. Sisters aren't supposed to remind you of things that happened when you were, like, four years old. "Oh, come on . . ." I start to say, but it's already too late. She's off and running with that memory.

"Remember? You saw this pregnant woman standing in line, and you said, 'Look, Mommy. That woman has a watermelon under her shirt.' Then when Mom tried to explain to you that the woman had a baby in her stomach, you wanted to know why anyone would want a baby watermelon under her shirt." She's laughing so hard that I can't help smiling a little myself.

But I resent it.

"That's when Mom decided to buy that funny book for us that was all about how babies were made. A little late for me. But at least you stopped asking about watermelons under women's shirts."

I remain unconvinced. She can tell. When she starts in on her next memory, I wish I had just gone along with her and said, "Sure, I'm an idiot. Gabe with his arm around Dana is obviously no big deal." But since I didn't, I have to sit through Kristen's next attempt to convince me that I suck at drawing the right conclusions from circumstances.

"And then there's that time you stole a candy bar from Walgreens. As soon as we got out to the van, some police car went by with its sirens and lights going. You thought he was coming for you, so you threw yourself at Mom and surrendered the candy bar while begging her not to let the police take you away to jail."

"This isn't the same thing at *all*. I'm not four anymore."

"I've got bad news for you: Seventeen and in love isn't any smarter."

This from someone who's been happily married for all of a year. Could she be any more condescending? I'm about to tell her that, but my cell phone starts playing "Für Elise."

"Aren't you going to get that?" Kristen asks when—duh—it becomes obvious that I'm *not*. What if it's Gabe? I just can't talk to him right now.

The phone keeps beeping out Beethoven. Then stops. Then starts again.

"For God's sake, Maddy. Answer it."

"No."

She digs around in my purse and pulls it out. "It's Gabe. Answer it."

Hello?! Who does she think I'm trying to *avoid* right now—Santa Claus? Kristen's managed to tick me off so much in the last few minutes that I'm not crying anymore.

She rolls her eyes at me—as if *I'm* the one being unreasonable here?—and answers the phone herself. I can only hear half the conversation, but Kristen's not dumb. She figures out how to let me in on the other half.

"Sandra told you you're in trouble? . . . You really are . . . Yeah, she saw you with your arm around—what's her name? Dana? . . . I know you're crazy about my sister and she's being an ass . . . Of course she's jumping to conclusions. . . ."

Enough is enough. I grab the phone from Kristen, who—I hate it when she does this—grins at me knowingly.

She walks away to give us some privacy as I say into the phone, "Okay, I'm here."

Gabe jumps straight to the explanation. Smart guy. He's got seconds before I hang up on him. "Maddy, chill out. I swear, what you saw didn't mean anything. Dana just got accepted to an acting program that she's been trying to get into for two years. It means she'll get to go to Europe this summer. I was just congratulating her."

This is supposed to make me feel better? I swear Dana is evil. She has it in for me, has ever since I started going out with Gabe. She's definitely still in love with him. And she does all these little things to get back at me. Every time I walk down the hall with Sandra and pass her and her friends, this nasty laughter breaks out. She also drew a disgusting caricature of me (how unfair can it be that she has all this artistic talent she uses to hurt people?) and hung it on my locker. It was a *totally* disgusting drawing. I blush every time I even think about it. I ripped the picture off my locker, but there Dana was, standing just a few lockers down, smugly smiling at me. On top of that, I've been getting these strange prank phone calls. They must be coming from her. No one else hates me enough to call and then hang up on me. Thank God she only has my home phone number and can't do the same thing to me on my cell.

So why, exactly, should I be happy that Dana the Demon can get my boyfriend to physically congratulate her? And exactly why should I be reassured that she's becoming an even better actress? It's hard enough to get Gabe to understand how awful she treats me at school. She puts on a completely different persona around him. She becomes gee-I'm-such-a-sweet-girl-who's-dealing-so-well-with-our-breakup-let's-continue-to-be-best-friends-forever. And he believes her. Well, mostly. He says he knows she can be mean sometimes, but he also claims that underneath all that she's a nice girl.

Right.

Rottweiler nice.

I can't even tell Gabe how I feel about Dana because he just doesn't get it. I guess that makes me feel even worse about the whole thing because I think that's the *only* thing about my feelings that he doesn't understand.

So how, exactly, am I supposed to react to this hey-isn't-it-great-that-you've-just-misinterpreted-the-whole-situation news?

Stymied, I opt for silence.

"Maddy?"

Still opting for silence.

"Maddy?"

My throat is killing me now. I'm going to start crying again. I don't want Gabe to know it, so I hit END and set the phone on the picnic table.

Ten seconds later, "Für Elise" starts up again. I let the song run for a second, and then I just can't bear the pain I know I'm causing Gabe, so I open it.

"Why'd you do that?" he asks. He sounds hurt, not angry.

"I was going to cry. Still am. Didn't want you to know."

And then, there it is . . . all those mortifying tears.

"Madison, c'mon. I love *you*. We've been going out now for a year. In all that time, I've never once thought about going back to Dana. If I had, you'd know it. I'd be with her. But I'm not, am I? I'm with you. And that's where I want to stay."

Ohmygod. Now there's a torrent of tears. Somehow I'm feeling both better and worse. Better because I know he's right. Worse because I've been stupid.

"Where are you, Maddy? I want to come be with you."

"I'm . . . at . . . the . . . p-park . . . near . . . m-my house."

"Stay put. I'll be there in ten minutes."

"No," I say. "Let's meet . . . at Kristen's house." I know she'll give us whatever privacy we need.

"All right," he agrees.

I flip the phone closed again, then walk off toward the merry-go-round, where Kristen is waiting for me.

school peas

age 11

Sandra stands up too suddenly. Her coat sleeve is under my tray, and as she tries to pull it out, the whole tray starts to flip. My plate slides across the tray, hitting the raised lip and coming to an abrupt stop.

The peas on top of it, though, continue their journey. They roll right off the plate and onto the table. Some travel as far as the table edge and then take a suicidal plunge to the floor.

Who can resist squashing underfoot one of the most despicable foods known to humankind? Don't get me wrong. I don't have anything against peas, actually. I don't even mind the taste of them.

But school peas? Those are an entirely different thing. They're always overcooked and mushy, and if that's not bad enough, they taste like a metal can that's been boiled.

So there's no way Sandra and I are going to resist the urge to smoosh them. We're immediately in a mad scramble to stomp on my peas. It's sort of like playing a video game . . . see it, stomp it . . . see it, stomp it . . . see it—

Are there any adults watching? Nope? Then stomp some more.

We both aim for the same pea, and my foot lands on top of hers. "Ouch!" I say.

Which is funny, because I'm the one who stomped on her. Isn't she the one who's supposed to have the hurt foot? We crack up and then start shushing each other.

Which makes me laugh even harder, because she accidentally spits on me when she's making the *shh* sound.

"Dis*gust*ing," I say, pulling away from her and knocking my chocolate milk off the table.

Which is hilarious, because now Sandra has a poop-colored splash on her shirtsleeve. She's trying to say something, but she's laughing so hard she can't get any words out.

Which is the funniest thing yet because . . . well, because *every*thing is funny right now. This is what I love about having Sandra as my best friend. My stomach hurts, my cheeks ache, I think I'm going to pee my pants, and there's nothing I want to do more than keep killing myself with laughter this way.

Uh-oh. We've shown up on the GPS of one of the lunch supervisors: TROUBLE AT TABLE 4. She's on her way over here.

Still giggling, Sandra starts mopping up chocolate milk with a napkin. I launch myself under the table and start trying to herd in the peas.

I hit my head on the table.

Which is funny, because . . . gosh, who even knows?

"What are you two doing?" the lunch supervisor demands.

"Uh . . . cleaning up?" Sandra says.

"You'd better be. It's a mess over here."

"We are," I assure her through my laughter.

"And stop giggling. You'll just make more of a mess." She glares at us as she moves off.

"Gee," I say after she's out of earshot, "who put lemon juice in her Cheerios this morning?"

Now we're almost choking on our giggles.

Until I see Tammy Havers looking over at us . . . wistfully. She's sitting at another table with some other girls. But the look she gives me makes me feel guilty. I can tell Tammy misses eating lunch with me this year.

I have nothing against her, I just want to sit with Sandra. It's really our only chance to have best-friend time together. We wouldn't be able to laugh together this way if there were other people around.

But I know that Tammy feels shut out. And I know that I *should* invite her to eat lunch with Sandra and me more often.

"Do you have all the peas picked up?" Sandra asks me. "Let's go play basketball until class starts."

"All except the ones that are squashed. And I'm *not* picking those up."

"Really, Madison," Sandra says in her best Ms. Henderson voice. Ms. Henderson is our math teacher, and she doesn't like me. I don't know why. But Sandra figured out on the third day of school how to imitate Ms. Henderson's voice. She's good at it. "And who will clean up after you? Do you think others were put on this Earth to clean up your messes?"

"No, Ms. Henderson," I say. "But I'm still not picking them up. They're disgusting. Give me detention if you want," I fire over my shoulder as I head toward the gym. I can feel Tammy watching me as I go.

$$\boxed{\text{i s}}$$

THIS STUPID PINECONE . . .

I'm frustrated enough to imagine myself smashing it into pieces.

But it still doesn't take me anywhere.

pain's greater plan

age 11

And I can put this here, I say to myself, unzipping the center pocket of my backpack and placing my new school planner inside. I'm going to be so organized this year. I've already put my whole class schedule into the grid at the front of the book. And if I ever need to know whether I'm supposed to be using the word *affect* or *effect*, I can just flip to the back of the planner and . . . there it will be.

Next, I unzip the front pocket and toss in my magnetized locker mirror. Getting ready for the first day of school is . . . nerve-racking.

My stomach is in knots. Middle school is a whole new thing. Will I like it? Will I get lost in this new, bigger building? How much more homework are the teachers going to give us? Will I be able to keep up with it all?

I don't actually want to go to middle school. I liked fifth grade. I knew everyone. I knew where everything was. I got good grades. I'm supposed to be excited to be moving up to a bigger school . . . dances and school sports, all that.

No, thanks.

At least I've got a planner to help me stay organized, right? At least I will if I manage not to lose it—the way I seem to lose everything.

I'd better check, just to make sure it's where I think it is . . . but—

It. Isn't. There. Where is it? Where? Where? *Where?!*

I frantically start unzipping pockets. Not there. Not in this one. I swear I put it in this pocket. Really. I *swear*.

"Mommmm!" I'm yelling. "Come here! I need you!"

I hear her charging up the stairs, and then she's standing in the doorway. "What is it?" she asks.

"I can't find my new planner."

She laughs. "And here I thought you actually needed something."

I hate it when she does that. Gets sarcastic, I mean. And I hate it even *more* when she acts like things that are really, *really* important don't matter at all.

"I already put the names and numbers of all my friends in it," I tell her, and then I burst into tears.

"Oh, honey," Mom says. She comes into the room and sits on my bed, sighing. "Where did you see it last?"

"I thought I put it in my backpack. Just a few minutes ago. And now it's gone." I wipe at tears rolling onto my cheeks. I can't stand the way my face feels all tight if I let tears dry on it.

"Maddy," Mom says, "I don't think you're truly crying over that planner."

"I *am*," I insist, sniffling. I suddenly wish I hadn't asked Mom for help. I can tell from the look on her face that she's about to tell me how she thinks I'm actually feeling.

As if she would know.

"It's always been hard for you to make changes, sweetie, and this is a pretty big change. All-new building. New people from other elementary schools. Teachers you've never seen before."

"I don't have trouble making changes," I protest. At least I won't if I have a planner.

Mom makes some kind of noise that sounds suspiciously like a . . . snort.

"Cut it out. Are you going to help me or what?"

She changes the subject. "All that sadness you're feeling right now, and all that fear you have about whether everything is going to be okay . . . all that is good, Maddy. You should want to feel that way."

Right. It's official. My mother is crazy.

"The way you're feeling right now makes you appreciate all the good times you have. All the pain of change and loss . . . those make you realize how much you love the things you have. Emily Dickinson wrote a poem about that, you know."

Oh, please. Emily Dickinson? My mother and her poets drive me crazy. None of my friends have parents who run around pulling out poetry for every occasion. Shakespeare, Dickinson, Frost, Eliot . . . sometimes I just want to scream when Mom starts reading me poetry. I mean, it was okay when it was about the cat, the fiddle, and a cow jumping over the moon, but now it's all this deep stuff she reads to me, and she expects me to connect it to my life.

I scramble to think of something I can say to distract her, but I'm not fast enough. Mom's already saying, "I'll just go find that book. . . ." She's on her way out the door.

Why did I ever ask her for help in the first place?

I start looking for my planner again, but all too soon Mom is back. "Here it is," she says excitedly. "'For each ecstatic instant / We must an anguish pay / In keen and quivering ratio / To the ecstasy.'"

She looks at me as if I'm supposed to *get* this.

"See what I mean?" Mom asks.

"No. What's ecstasy?" I ask.

Now she's laughing. As if any of this is funny?

"It means extreme happiness. Giddy happiness. The best happiness in the world. She's saying that for every moment of wonder and excitement, you have to pay with an equal amount of pain."

Somehow, this doesn't seem fair. I don't understand why God would make you pay for your happiness with pain. Seems like we should just get to be happy. I tell Mom this.

"Hmmm . . ." she says. "I can see why you might think that'd be nice. Maybe the word *pay* isn't quite the right description of it. I don't think it's an exchange like that. It's more that . . . well, the two emotions are connected. They are one thing. And in coming together they make each other what they are. Without pain, you wouldn't understand happiness. And without happiness, you wouldn't feel the pain."

"Let's just get rid of all happiness and feel nothing if it means we don't have to feel pain," I say.

"You might find that boring," Mom says as she starts opening all the pockets of my backpack. Then she's laughing again and pulling out my new planner. "Here it is."

"You found it!" I shriek, reaching for it in excitement.

"Just think . . . if you hadn't experienced all those bad feelings about losing this, you wouldn't get to feel this way right now," Mom says, handing me—

———

Yeah. I get Mom's point now. I think I have ever since I started going back to the Daddy-Daughter Dance. The loss of that ticket brought pain but also joy.

The Universe wants me to understand that I do have some choices. One of the most important ones is whether I accept painful moments and move beyond them. Forcing pain out of life isn't always the right choice.

How come my mother (not to mention Emily Dickinson) got to figure all this out while she was still alive?

I had to be dead to get it.

witch's nails

age 12

"I wish I could get these stupid nails to stay on my fingers," I tell Sandra and her grandmother.

"Yeah, well, at least you don't have to wear this idiotic wig. It feels like I've got a boat balancing up there."

"And my hat's supposed to be any better?"

We both break out in laughter. We might be complaining, but we can't wait to get out there and trick-or-treat. Years of Halloween have already provided us with standard procedures regarding candy trades. We both keep all the M&M's we get because we love them. But SweeTarts always go to Sandra. I hate them so much, I never even ask for a trade. Now, Tootsie Rolls, though, I like enough to demand an exchange for. I get her Snickers bars for them since Sandra hates peanuts.

We're in the living room showing our costumes to Sandra's grandmother before we take off for the evening. She hugs us both. "Y'all sure look terrific," she drawls.

Sandra's grandmother is fantastic. I'm glad, too. With the mother Sandra has, she deserves to have—and does have—the best grandmother in the world. I just don't get it, though. How could this wonderful woman have been the parent of Sandra's mother? It's like trying to get your mind around the possibility that Mary Poppins could be the mother of Cruella De Vil.

Grandma Belle, as Sandra calls her (that's short for Bellerue, her grandmother's last name), is a true Southern lady. The most important thing in her life is her family, and she'll do anything to make them happy. I get to see quite a bit of her because Mrs. Simpson is always sick (or at least she thinks she is), so Grandma Belle will fly up to Michigan and take care of Sandra and Mrs. Simpson whenever her daughter complains that she has the littlest headache. Mr. Simpson is polite to her, although Sandra thinks her dad doesn't actually like having Grandma Belle around quite so much.

I can't see how *anyone* could not want Grandma Belle

around. She makes marvelous cookies, and she compliments Sandra and me at least twenty times a day. She just sort of makes me happy to be alive. She's always expected me to call her Grandma Belle, too, so I do.

"I'd look better if these nails would stay on my fingers," I complain.

Grandma Belle picks one of the long green nails off my finger and examines the cheap adhesive on its back. "*Hhmpf*," she grunts. "I'll just find us some glue, Madison, for those nails of yours. That'll take care of them. They'll stay on when Grandma Belle's finished with them." She temporarily sticks the nail back on my finger.

We hear her rummaging around in the kitchen. I try to straighten Sandra's clown wig. It's sliding off to the left, and strands of her curly hair are starting to escape. "How about a bobby pin?" I ask. "Maybe that'll keep it on."

I'd volunteer to go up and get one out of the bathroom for her, but Mrs. Simpson is upstairs lying down because—of course—she's just not feeling well. Another mystery ailment that the doctor can't identify. When I went up there to get something ten minutes ago, she emerged from the bedroom and said, "My, what a lot of noise you can manage to make, Madison." Then she looked me up and down and said with a Southern drawl, "What a great witch you are."

And let me tell you, that *wasn't* intended as a Halloween compliment. Somewhere along the line, Mrs. Simpson learned the art of using a compliment to deliver underhanded insults. She's the queen of it. And she manages to use a tone of voice that really lets you know that you're being insulted behind words that otherwise seem harmless, even friendly.

I can still hear Grandma Belle out in the kitchen rummaging around for the glue. Then the intercom on the phone buzzes. Grandma Belle drops everything and runs upstairs. Her daughter needs her.

"Forget the nails," Sandra tells me. "Let's just go."

She hands me a pillowcase for what I hope is going to be the mother lode of candy. That's when I notice that another one of my green nails has fallen off. "Oh, skunk!" I say. "Another one's gone."

Sandra and I get down on the floor to look for the nail, but we can't find it. After a few minutes, I say, "Oh, just forget it. Let's go."

I rip off all the other witch's nails, too, and leave them sitting on the coffee table in the living room.

Maybe Mrs. Simpson will want them for the finishing touches on the costume she should be wearing every day.

age 17

My arm gets tangled up in the phone cord as I'm trying to hang it up.

Stupid thing . . .

Stupid school policy, too. Why can't we just use our cell phones? It would be so much easier for me to call my mother on that than to have to get a pass from a teacher to use the office phone. . . .

Stupid . . . oh, all right . . . stupid me. I wouldn't even be making a phone call if I had remembered to bring my homework to school. I've just had to listen to Mom drone on and on about how she was *not* happy to discover she'd have to leave work, drive home to pick up my homework, and bring it back to me . . . all by sixth hour. I'm certain to have to listen to more of the same over dinner tonight, too.

I grunt out my frustration as I pull my arm out of the super-long, must-be-able-to-go-anywhere-in-the-office phone cord. Vice Principal Patterson's office door opens, and the air current whisks my pass right off the counter and onto the floor of the forbidden territory lying beyond the Great Counter Divide.

Must have pass to go back to class.

Must not cross the border into the sovereign territory of principals and secretaries.

Now what?

Wait . . . why are the cops coming out of Mr. Patterson's office? This does not look good.

Tammy follows the police, and Mr. Patterson brings up the rear.

This looks even worse. Somehow, Tammy's gotten caught. The question is, at what? She's done enough illegal stuff that it's anyone's guess. But mine is the whole drug thing.

My great deductive skills are confirmed when she catches my eye as she walks through the gate separating the Land of Office Staff and the Land of Students. Her eyes flash at me with something so . . . feral . . . I'm terrified. Maybe she's smarter than to threaten my life verbally in front of the police, but she communicates effectively with her eyes. The message *You're dead* stabs me with knifelike force.

I swallow.

I look away.

Tammy follows the policeman out of the office, but even as the door closes behind them, I can still feel Tammy's eyes on me through the glass window between the office and the hall. She thinks I've told someone about what I saw in the bathroom a few weeks ago.

"Can I help you?" one of the secretaries asks me.

Probably not. Unless you're good in hand-to-hand combat. Or have a weapon I can use to protect myself. "Ummm," I say, "my pass? It fell onto the floor on that side. I need it to get back to class."

She glances around at the floor. "I don't see it here. Are you sure it fell on *this* side?"

"Yeah."

She looks around for a few more seconds and then gives up and writes me a new one.

All in all, I'm glad it's taken a little extra time to clear up the pass issue. It's pretty certain that the police have gotten Tammy out of the building by now.

I'd rather not see her at the moment.

baby doll

"Mommy, play. Now!"

"It's time to go to sleep now, Madison. Lie down. I'll cover you up. See the Pooh Bear blanket? He's waiting to cover you up."

"I standing up!"

"I know you're standing up. Lie down now and go to sleep."

"Play. I play now."

"No, it's sleepy time now. We'll play tomorrow. There's a good girl. Lie down now. See how nice it is when Pooh

Bear covers you up? I love you, sweetie. I'll see you in the morning."

"Need Baby Sarah. Give me Baby."

"She's right there at the foot of the bed."

"Give Baby Sarah. I want Baby. Please give Baby me."

"Here you go. Here's Baby Sarah."

"Baby Sarah bad. She not eat all dinner."

"She didn't? You didn't eat all your dinner, either, did you? Maybe Baby will be good tonight, though, and go right to sleep."

"Baby no sleep. Baby play. Maddy playing, too."

"Night-night, Maddy."

"All gone Mommy. Baby, Mommy all gone. We play now. I stand up, Baby. When we eat dinner . . . when we . . . Baby Sarah cry. Say I don't want dinner. I don't like carrots. Daddy say eat. Daddy say carrots good and make Maddy grow. Like milk. Milk make my grow, too, Baby. But me and Baby said no.

"I laying down Baby. We sleep. Bad Baby. Time to go sleep now. But play instead. Time out, Baby Sarah. Time out. Sit there, Baby. Still playing, Baby. But time out. Bad Baby go under bed. Time out.

"Now, Baby, be good baby. Sleep. Baby sleep . . . 'cause me a good girl . . ."

———

". . . Today I go to babysitter house . . . Mommy take me. But I not cry. Mommy come back . . ."

"How's my sweetie this morning? Time to get up and go. We'll have a good breakfast this morning. How about some pancakes?"

"Pancakes yes. Maddy love pancakes. Baby. Where Baby Sarah? Baby breakfast too."

"I don't know where your baby is, Maddy. She was in bed with you last night. I don't see her. Let's look under the covers . . . No. She's not there. Behind your pillow? Not there, either. We can find her later, sweetie. We have to get ready to leave now or Mommy will be late for work. Come on. . . . Oh, you're getting heavy to carry."

"Want Baby now . . . want Baby now. Baby can't find—"

Not so freaky as going all the way back to being a baby.

But still.

Definitely freaky enough. I mean, it's like I know what's happening but also like I *don't* know what's happening. Worth a second try . . .

. . . And a third try . . .

I'm not sure what fascinates me about being two again. The feel of that wet diaper in the morning? So *not* that. It's almost enough to keep me from going back there. But not quite.

It must be the way it feels to have Mom pick me up and carry me away from my bed. Or the feel of falling, falling, falling asleep.

Traveling back to two is way less disconcerting than going back to infancy. I can at least name things while I'm two. I think that's why the baby experience disturbed me so much. No language there.

This realization helps me understand how being dead now is different than, well, the last time I wasn't alive. There had to be such a time, right? I mean, there was a time before I was born, and my body wasn't alive then, but I must have had a soul, an energy, a *something* in existence. I couldn't have come from, well, *nowhere*, could I? According to physics, energy is never created or destroyed. I'm a form of energy, so I must have existed in some form before life.

Only, back then I don't think I knew that I existed. Because I didn't have language. I guess the reward for having gone through a whole lifetime is gaining language. Here in *Is* I still get to use words. Silently only, maybe. But I still have them.

I guess I'm an *old* soul now.

Or maybe just not a new one.

Makes me realize how powerful words are. They have some kind of miraculous ability to make me who I am.

Or *was*.

No, *am*. Because I still have them.

photo in the wind

age 17

The scrapbook and folder of pictures is slipping around in my arms. Too much stuff. I'm bound to drop it and lose half my pictures in this ridiculous wind. I should have accepted Gabe's help carrying all this into the house.

Too late now. He's pulling out of the driveway.

What's that on the front porch? It's right in my way. I'm not sure I can manage to step over it while juggling all this—

"Ohmygod!" I scream, dropping everything. I don't care what happens to it.

Words cannot express the explosion of emotion erupting from me. It escapes in hysterical screams. I hear them. They're *loud* but not loud enough to release this surge of emotion. That's all I can do: release it. So I throw every bit of my being into screaming louder, screaming from somewhere deep inside me that I didn't even know existed.

Gabriel's tires screech on the cement as he pulls back into the drive. From somewhere far away, I process that he's coming, running toward me, so I stop screaming and start crying as he reaches for me and wraps me in his arms. "It's okay, it's okay," he's saying as he presses my face to his shoulder and strokes my hair, but then he's swearing— gently, softly. An obscene lullaby takes shape as he alternates between reassuring me and expressing his shock in four-letter words.

My horror converts to anger, and I push away from him, saying, "It's not okay. It's not. She's dead. Cozy's dead."

And the worst is that "dead" doesn't even begin to describe what she is.

Mutilated . . .

Broken . . .

Crushed . . .

Blood around her head has matted her hair in clumps. Her legs, broken, are arranged in an unnatural shape. Her tail, that once-proud flag proclaiming her cathood, is limp and bent. The saddest thing I notice is the dried blood that trickled from her mouth at the end. That same mouth with the scratchy sandpaper tongue she used so many times to lick ice cream off my fingers.

"Who'd do this?" I choke out around sobs, pulling away from Gabe.

"No one," Gabe says. "At least not on purpose. It was an accident. She must've gotten hit by a car."

I can't tell if he's trying to protect me or if he's actually this stupid. Either way, I'm not putting up with it.

I turn my back to Cozy. I can't stand to see her as I confront the universe with this cruelty. "She's not in the road, Gabe. If she'd been hit by a car, she'd be in the road."

"Maybe a neighbor—"

"She's *arranged*, Gabe. Posed. Someone wanted us to see her this way." I discover that I'm whispering, trying to protect Cozy, for God's sake, as if I don't want her to hear the truth about what's happened to her. As if she doesn't already know. She was there.

But still I whisper. "A neighbor wouldn't stick her on the porch for us to . . . to stumble over."

"Maddy, I'm sorry. I know you loved her."

"I've loved her for ten years. Why? Who hates us enough to kill our cat?"

"I don't know what happened here, Madison. But I just can't believe that someone . . . someone . . . y'know—"

"Killed her, Gabe. Someone killed her."

"No, Maddy, I don't think so. It's bizarre, you're right, finding her here like this, but it has to be that someone was stupid enough not to realize this isn't how you bring someone's cat back after it's been hit by a car. Some kid, maybe, who doesn't know any better. C'mon."

What he's saying makes a whole lot more sense than what I'm thinking. I let him pull me back into his arms. I want to believe him.

But I just can't.

The air around me seems to mold itself into an ominous shape. It presses against me so hard that I can barely breathe. I've become prey to a new feeling I've never experienced before. Something out there is tracking me down. I can feel it. Something has caught the scent of my blood. And I don't know how to escape it, because I don't have any idea which direction the threat is coming from.

Gabe kisses my forehead.

"I never figured out what her third name was," I whisper, holding him even tighter.

"What?"

I can tell he thinks I'm losing it. Maybe I am. "Never mind," I say. I wish he understood what I meant, but I don't have the energy to explain Mom and T. S. Eliot's theory about cat names—or that I've caught Cozy over the years contemplating this secret she's managed to keep from me.

Gabe whispers, "Go in the house. Call your mom and

dad. I'll pick up all those photos and come in to sit with you."

I do what he tells me.

Because I can't look at Cozy again.

Because even though I don't care about my scrapbook right now, I know I will someday.

But mostly I do because I'm afraid that whatever is stalking me will return, and I'm scared to stay out here any longer. I step through the front door, expecting my house's crisp scent of eucalyptus to offer some comfort. But it doesn't. I sense that the house is grieving the loss of Cozy, too.

Is feels emptier than it ever has when I return this time, but at least I'm feeling some hope. Maybe Cozy never did actually know what happened to her in those final moments. After all, I don't know what happened in my final moments.

And now I realize something important: Maybe I shouldn't want to know so badly what happened to me. I remember that trickle of blood matted along Cozy's jaw, and then I recall the oppressive feeling of being stalked that hit me just before I went into the house. I'm afraid that whatever was stalking me . . . found me.

What if . . .

What if my predator caught Gabriel in its net, too?

It's an appalling thought.

God, if you're out here somewhere amid all this clut-
ter from my life, please tell me that whatever happened to
Gabriel, it wasn't *that*.

the ring

"You're paranoid," Gabe says.

"I am *not!*" This whole home-alone-with-Gabe thing isn't going the way I thought it would. Here I am, with my boyfriend, in my own room where we could be comfortably horizontal on the bed together, no parents barging in (they're with Kristen, helping her paint the baby's room), and what are we doing? Fighting.

"You are, too," Gabe says. "This is just silly."

Okay, being told I'm silly and paranoid? This takes me to an all-new level of anger. It isn't helping any that I'm still shaking from the car accident—even if it was three hours ago. I was so upset right after it happened that my parents weren't going to leave me alone to go do the painting at Kristen's. I convinced them to go, thinking time alone with Gabe would help me more than hanging out with my parents would, but now he's not even concerned about the way his ex-girlfriend almost killed me.

More than that . . . he's defending her.

"You weren't there, Gabe. I'm not being silly and paranoid. I'm telling you, she hit me on purpose. We were both stopped at a stop sign. I had the right of way. She looked *directly* at me and then drove that Mercedes straight into the driver's side of my car. She *wanted* to hurt me."

"That doesn't even make sense. Why would she mess up her parents' car?"

"Uh, hello? Because she wants to hurt me? Because she still wants you back?"

"Jesus, Maddy. You and I have been together for a year and a half now. It's not like she would think I'm going to go running back to her anytime soon. And hitting you with a car wouldn't do anything to get her back with me anyway, unless she killed you or something. She's not a murderer. You're the one who's jeal—"

He's just admitted that he'd go back to her if I were dead, and he thinks he can accuse me of being silly? "See?! You just admitted you'd get back with her if I were dead!"

"I did *not*! How crazy can you get, Maddy? You know that's not at all what I meant! Your jealousy is driving me insane. You've never been able to let go of thinking that I still have a thing for her. No matter what I do, I can't get you to let go of that."

"Well, gee, Gabe, it might help if you'd stop defending her. Maybe then I'd believe that you cared about me more than you do her."

"I do! But I'm not going to believe that Dana hit you on purpose with her parents' Mercedes. Sometimes she's awful. I admit it. But she's not that crazy. And she isn't trying to kill you."

Okay, I start crying. I can't explain to him how . . . insecure I've felt since we found Cozy dead on the front porch a few weeks ago. That strange sense of being hunted hasn't gone away. It's just intensified. And today, as Dana was pulling that car straight into me, it was like my predator finally caught me. Time seemed to slow, to laugh at the way I'd been captured.

"This isn't just me being paranoid or jealous, Gabe. I mean it. She wants me dead. I think she even killed Cozy."

The strangest look crosses his face. It's terrifying to me because I can tell he thinks I've gone off the deep end on this one. I feel more alone than I've ever been in my life. And all those feelings roil inside me with anger. How dare he not believe me? I thought he loved me.

I grab a small ring off my vanity (I'd use something bigger if it were in reach) and whip it at him where he's standing in the doorway.

The I-don't-know-this-girl look that crosses his face is too much. I'm humiliated. He's right—I *am* psycho right now. I owe him an apology, and yet, even though I know this, and even though humiliation has just been added to the emotional stew I've been cooking, I feel like I hate Gabe right now.

And I hate him even more when he turns on his heel and simply walks away from me. His feet pound quickly down the stairs, and then I hear the front door slamming.

Still crying, I wander over to the doorway and get down on my hands and knees to start searching for the missing ring. It isn't valuable or anything. It's just a ring that my grandma gave me for my twelfth birthday. But it seems incredibly important that I find it right now. I've lost so much else—my cat, my boyfriend, my sanity. I can't bear to lose this ring, too. It feels as if finding it might help me find all the other things I've lost.

Something metal brushes against—

losing myself at disney world

age 6

Hot . . . hot . . . hot. The sun beats down on us. I love the Magic Kingdom, but I'm tired of the heat and just plain exhausted. The sun glares off of everything. And my face feels gritty with sweat. My hair is soaked. Mom and Dad have even decided that we all need popcorn to replace some of the salt we've lost from sweating.

I like that idea.

I take a piece of popcorn and drop it, watching it fall. It seems to float slowly in the heavy air. When it finally hits the ground, I kick it with my foot. This place is so glittering and clean, I'm happy to see the lonely popcorn piece on the ground.

"But I want to go back on the Big Thunder Mountain Railroad ride," Kristen moans.

I kick the piece of popcorn along as we walk. This is one of my favorite things to do. Walk . . . kick . . . walk . . . kick . . .

"We will," Mom reassures her. "But your father wants to take you on the Jungle Cruise first."

"You said we could go through the Pirates of the Caribbean ride again," I whine. I feel betrayed. I give my popcorn piece an extra-hard kick. It skitters off and I lose sight of it.

This. Is. It.

The end of the world. It's too hot. I don't want to see anything else except the Pirates of the Caribbean ride, where it's dark and cool. I'm tired. My eyes hurt. My feet hurt. My head aches.

And now I've lost a piece of popcorn.

A piece that was very important to me.

I can't help it. I begin to cry.

My family hasn't even noticed that they've left me behind. They keep right on walking. Fine . . . if they don't care about me, then I don't care about them, either. I'll run away and live in the Swiss Family Treehouse that we saw earlier today. All by myself. Forever.

Only . . . that's not sounding quite so great now that I

can't even see my family anymore.

I panic.

I start crying even harder.

Suddenly, Mom and Dad are standing in front of me. "Madison, stay with us!" my mother starts to chastise me, but then she notices how hard I'm crying, so she wipes my face with a Kleenex instead. "C'mon, sweetie," she says. She reaches for my hand and pulls. I yank my hand away from hers.

"What is it, honey?" Daddy asks.

"My popcorn," I wail.

"It's right there in your hand," Daddy tries to reassure me, gesturing to the bucket I'm still holding.

"No," I explain through my sobs. "I was kicking a piece and I lost it."

A strange silence descends between them, even as all the noise of the Magic Kingdom surrounds us.

Then Mom says something really strange to Dad. I hear something that sounds like "object attachment." Even though I don't understand those words, I know Mom's tone of voice. It's the one she uses when what she *really* means is "Maddy's difficult. I can't wait until she's older"—even if those aren't the words she's saying.

"C'mon, sweetheart," Daddy says. "I'll give you a piggyback ride."

I climb on Daddy's back, and we move on toward Cinderella's Castle.

$$\boxed{\text{is}}$$

MOM'S COMMENT about "object attachment" suddenly makes perfect sense. I've always had some kind of connection to the things I've owned. Losing them left me feeling bereft because they were linked to everyone and everything in my life that was important. And unlike the people I loved, I could control them—at least I could when I wasn't losing them.

Objects are safe, too. I mean, they don't change much. A pen stays a pen and a set of keys always unlocks something. You can go back to the object, hold it, remember who you were when you loved it. That's something you can count on.

But let's face it, I'm not talking about "you" right now. I'm talking about me.

The same me who—even in death—is incredibly attached to these things because they take me back to who I was. Somehow, though, it doesn't seem quite as fulfilling as it once did to have a relationship with a piece of popcorn that I'm kicking along on the pavement . . .

Kicking . . . I suddenly realize I haven't tried that yet with the pinecone. I've imagined myself doing every other possible thing that can be done with it. But I never envisioned myself kicking it as I walked along. Could that be . . . ?

I swim myself through the currents of space until I find the pinecone, and . . .

the pinecone

"What am I going to do, Maddy?" Sandra asks.

I kick the pinecone along as we walk down the trails of the park. I know I need to get out of my head, where the image of Gabe's and my fight last week is on automatic replay 24-7. We still haven't talked to each other, and I can't stop wondering if this is the end of our relationship. Our gazes have met across the hallway several times, and I keep wanting to go up and tell him how sorry I am that I threw that ring at him.

But I just can't. I guess it's the humiliation. And the

fear . . . that he won't accept my apology. And—let's face it, I'm still angry at him, too, about Dana.

I keep expecting to see him walking down the hall with her or something.

Only—thank God—he doesn't.

He just looks at me like he wants to talk to me, too, but can't.

It's hard to stop thinking about all that and pay attention to Sandra. But I have to do it somehow. She needs me right now.

Some friend I am . . . only half concentrating on what she's saying.

And the thing is . . . the decision she makes about this whole mess is going to have an impact on me. What if I lose my best friend, too? I can't bear that. It almost makes me want to give her what I *know* is the wrong advice. Because if she does what's right, I *will* lose her.

Sure, if she moves to Oregon with her dad, she'll still email me and call. Even come to visit sometimes. But it won't be the same. Gradually the emotional distance between us will match the distance between Michigan and Oregon. The pain of that realization slices through my obsession with Gabriel and helps me concentrate on how important this really is.

"I don't want you to leave, Sandra. *I* want you to stay here with your mom, but your mom's . . . well, not quite right. You know that. How could you stand to live with her without your dad there to help you manage her?"

There ought to be a law that says parents can't get divorced during their kids' senior year of high school. They ought to have to stick it out until the kids are gone so they don't disrupt the most important year of our lives.

"But if I stayed," Sandra argues, "it'd only be for the rest of this year, right? I mean, in ten months I'll be going away to college."

"Sandra . . ." It's hard to figure out how to tell her this. She's always been so touchy when it comes to talking about her mother. There's a lot about her mom that she just won't admit to herself . . . like that her mother's a really sick woman—and I'm not talking physically. "I'm not sure that you'll *go* to college if you stay here with your mom."

"I'm going to college. There's no way I'm not!" she protests.

"Oh, I know you'll take college classes. But, well, I don't think you'll go *away* to college. I think your mom will manage to convince you to stay at home and go to community college. Or maybe she'll convince you to go part-time so you can commute to a university. But . . ." I kick the pinecone a little too hard, and it skitters off the path into the grass. I track it down but have to kick it a couple times to get it back onto the path. "Can you see your mom living alone?" I just know Mrs. Simpson will convince Sandra that leaving her alone will kill her.

"But how can I go off with Dad right now and leave her by herself? It's like she'd die. Maybe even kill herself."

Too late—obviously. Mrs. Simpson has already convinced Sandra she's responsible for the life and death of her mother.

Still, Sandra's comment shows progress—sort of. Sandra's never admitted before that her mom is *this* kind of unstable.

But a response to the comment is also tricky. I'm not sure exactly how to approach this subject, so I sound totally stupid as I talk in slow motion. "At least . . . if you go . . . now . . . you'll have, well, your dad . . . he'll help you get up the . . . courage . . . to do it. You'll have him . . . reassuring you that . . . well, that *you* need . . . a life, too. And if you . . . leave with him . . . won't your grandma . . . I mean . . . can't your mom . . . live with her parents? If you weren't here . . . maybe she'd . . . maybe she'd move back South . . . with them."

"She says she won't. She's going to stay right here, and she wants me to stay with her."

Great. Just great. It's like Mrs. Simpson has already anticipated all my moves and put her game pieces in place to defend against them. She's not a woman I ever want to play chess with.

Yet that seems to be exactly what I'm doing.

In frustration, I kick the pinecone too hard again, but

I'm so focused on Sandra that I don't pay much attention to where it's going. "See? That's what I mean. She'll do that to you again next year when it's time for you to go to college. Convince you that she'll be all alone if you leave." I want to tell her that her mother is seriously crazy, but my credibility in the judging-people's-sanity category has plunged to an all-time low. Even Sandra thinks it was nuts that I accused Dana of killing my cat and trying to kill me. Better that I not mention anything related to, well, mental health.

We're both silent for a moment as I look for the pine-cone off the path. I don't find it. Sighing, I sit down on the grass. Sandra's still standing, and as I gaze up at her, I notice that in the past few months she's gained weight. I'm surprised. How could I not have noticed until this moment that she's put on about fifteen pounds? Have I been that absorbed in my own life? She's lost that birdlike fragility I've always thought of her as having, and I mourn its loss— not because she's less pretty than she used to be, but because the difference in her shows me how much everything has been changing lately.

"She thinks you'll try to get me to stay, you know."

"What do you mean?" I ask, patting the ground next to me, encouraging her to sit.

She does. "Whenever we have this conversation at home, she tells me to ask you what to do. She thinks you'll try to get me to stay here with you."

I can just imagine *those* scenes. No doubt Sandra's mom is crying and pleading. She'll use any dirty tactic she can to keep Sandra tied to her. I'm glad I've managed to think about Sandra's best interests instead of my own for once. I know I'm selfish sometimes, but selfish enough to try to keep Sandra under the spell of her mother?

No. Not that selfish. I'd rather lose my best friend and have her get the chance to lead a somewhat healthy life than keep her near me if it means living with her mother.

"Don't get me wrong, Sandra. I wish you could stay. I wish your dad wouldn't leave. Couldn't he get a job around here?"

She shakes her head sadly. "He says he has to get away from her, too. And he wants me to go with him. He thinks, like you do, that it'll be bad for me to stay here with Mom. But I don't see how he can just walk away from her like that. She needs us. She's defenseless without us."

"Or she wants you to think she is. She doesn't have to be." I don't add that her mother is anything *but* defenseless. She's one of the strongest women I know. She uses the appearance of weakness to get people to do what she wants them to. "Much as I want you to stay here—and I definitely do, Sandra—I want even more for you to be happy. And you'd never be happy here alone in that house with your mom. You know that, don't you?"

"Yeah, I do," she admits. "It's just so hard to do what

I should. I'm terrified that—" She pauses for a moment, unsure. Then she plunges ahead. "She's been threatening to kill herself. I think she might really . . . this time . . . I mean now . . . How do I tell you all this? There's stuff I probably should have let you know before."

There's *more*?! I suddenly feel betrayed. I guess I shouldn't have assumed I knew everything about Sandra, even if she is my best friend, but still I don't like hearing that she's been keeping secrets from me. Especially about her mom.

When Sandra doesn't pick up the thread of her thoughts, I prompt her by using my knee to nudge hers.

"Well, it seems like my whole life she's been threatening to kill herself. The first time I remember it, I was in, like, first grade, I think. She started waving around a butcher knife while she was having some fight with Dad. Told him she'd kill herself."

It's not hard to figure out who won that fight, but I keep my mouth shut about it.

"When I went to camp during fourth grade, remember how I had to suddenly go home?"

"Yeah. Your mom got sick."

"Well, sort of. She called and told me she had this bottle of pills that made her feel better while I was gone, but she thought she'd need to take a lot of them to make all the pain go away. I only kind of got what she was hinting at, but I got it enough to know I was scared and had to go home."

There's a moment of silence between us. "How often?" I finally ask.

"How often what?"

"How often does she threaten to kill herself?"

"Oh, I don't know. Sometimes she'll go a couple years without ever threatening to kill herself. Then suddenly she'll be threatening her life every day for a couple weeks. Do you know how many different ways there are to kill yourself? I do. I think my mom's said she was going to use every one. The whole thing has always scared me, but not as much as it does right now. It's somehow different."

I doubt it. "How? How is it different?"

Sandra shakes her head. "I don't know. I can't explain it. It just is."

I put my arm around her and hug her. There's nothing I can say to make her less afraid. Right now I have to find strength I don't think I have to help support her through this. Her latest confessions have only made me more convinced that she *has* to go live with her dad in Oregon. "C'mon," I say. "Let's go swing."

She glances over at a row of swings where we used to play together when we were little. "Okay," she says.

We get up slowly and take off toward the swings.

physics

It's a beautiful fall day. Perfect for sitting outside the school to eat lunch. The leaves are all golden and orange, and a breeze is teasing them out of their branches so they fall swirling around my feet under the picnic table.

Too bad I can't enjoy the day's beauty. I'm miserable.

Miserable because I'm feeling lonely without Gabe. We still haven't said anything to each other since the fight about my car accident.

Miserable because Sandra didn't even come to school today. She must be that overwhelmed by the choice she has to make.

Miserable because I didn't manage to finish my physics homework and it's due in twenty minutes.

Miserable because my sister went into labor this morning, but my parents wouldn't let me go to the hospital with her. They insisted I should go to school, since first babies take such a long time to enter the world.

Can't say I blame babies for that. Who'd really want to enter this messed-up experience called life?

I'm so intent on all this that I don't realize at first that I've been playing with my necklace . . . the one that Gabe gave me last summer. It's silver, and in the center, it has block letters that spell out FOREVER.

Yeah. So much for that. We aren't even talking right now.

Tears blur my eyes. Then I'm startled by a soft touch on my shoulder. I jump and whirl around, gasping.

Gabe.

He holds up his hands in a classic "I'm innocent" gesture. "Didn't mean to startle you," he says.

"You didn't," I say, so desperate to be nice to him that it takes me a second to realize how *obviously* that's not true. "I mean," I stutter, "I mean, you did, but I'm glad you did."

We just gaze at each other for the longest time. Then he finally says, "Did you get number eleven?" He nods his head toward my physics homework. "I worked on that one for about a half hour last night and never did get it to come out right."

Great. Just great. And I have, what, twenty minutes to finish the whole assignment? But physics homework isn't what I want to be thinking about.

"I'm sorry. I mean, about that whole . . . fight. I shouldn't have thrown that ring at you. I guess I was way shook up by that accident." Okay, I don't think that's *actually* why I did it, but hey, I'll use just about any fair excuse right now.

"I know," he says. "I should have been cooler about the whole thing, too. All my frustration with the thing between you and Dana just hit crisis point."

He straddles the bench next to me, dumping his backpack onto the picnic table. "I've been trying for a week now to figure out what to say to you."

"Me too."

"It's just that . . . Maddy, I love you. I do. And I don't understand why you don't know it."

"Well, it's just that—"

"Don't," he interrupts. He holds a finger against my lips. His touch is so gentle, so cherishing that I know, somehow, that everything will be all right. "I know it would be easier for you if I just didn't have anything to do with Dana. But can't you understand she was a major part of my life for two years? I feel like you're asking me to throw away that time . . . completely. To write it off. I want to move forward with you, but I don't want to give up my past. And even though I know Dana can be a complete pain sometimes, I can't believe that I'd spend two years going out with someone who's the kind of monster you keep trying to convince me Dana is."

I look down at my physics homework. The wind is catching the edge of it, flipping up the bottom half. Only my cardboard container of uneaten french fries is holding it down. At the moment, it's easier to look at that paper than it is to meet Gabe's gaze. I feel so much . . . shame. Everything he's saying makes sense. But I don't know how to respond to it, because I still feel an intense fear of something, but I don't know what is. I'm not imagining bogeymen here. There's a real monster out there somewhere, and it's as likely to be Dana as anyone else.

And yet what if she is just a normal girl? What if she didn't purposefully cause that accident? Then who killed my cat?

"I'm not sure what to say, Gabe. I love you, too. I've been miserable without you the last week. I don't want to put you in a bad spot."

He puts his index finger under my chin and lifts it up. Then he kisses the corner of my mouth. It's a soft kiss, like the fluttering of a butterfly's wings, and I want more. I turn to face him and, putting my arms around him, lean in for a real kiss. Something greater than either of us seems to infuse that kiss with power.

"I'm sorry, Gabe," I say when we finish kissing. I'm

being deliberately vague because the truth is, I actually don't know what I'm sorry for. Maybe everything. And nothing. At the same time.

He leans his forehead against mine. I like the feel of his skin.

"I hope we don't ever fight again," I say.

He smiles wickedly. "The making-up part is pretty nice."

I grin.

He kisses me again.

Don't ask me why, but I remember the whole physics thing right then. Not that Gabe isn't the kind of kisser who can drive mundane thoughts of physics assignments right out of my head . . . because he is. But I'm pretty wound up today . . . everything from Kristen's baby to Sandra's problems are pounding at my consciousness. And for some bizarre reason, it's the physics assignment that wins the anxiety war.

"I don't suppose you want to help me with my physics," I say.

Another wicked grin. "I thought I *was* helping you with physics."

"Different form of physics. That one doesn't help my grade any in Mr. Martin's class."

He sighs. "Okay." He opens up his backpack and starts to pull out his book.

"Want to come with me after school today to check on Sandra?" I ask. I fill him in on how she's been struggling the last week to make this important decision. "Her father wants to move by early next week, so she's really stressed about what she's going to do."

Gabe whistles in commiseration. "Sure, I'll go over there with you."

"Oh, and Kristen went into labor this morning," I tell him.

"Hey, well, at least that's good news. Any word?"

"Not yet. I called my mom at the beginning of lunch, and she said the hospital sent Kristen home to wait it out a bit more. I heard that some first babies can take more than twenty-four hours to arrive, so I guess that means she'll give birth in the middle of the night or something."

"Hmm . . . October thirtieth seems like a good birthday to me."

"Yeah. Or the thirty-first if it's after midnight. Both are pretty good."

"Halloween baby."

I laugh. "Don't say that. It makes my niece—or nephew—sound like Satan's spawn."

"The ancient Celts believed that during this time of year the boundaries between the worlds of the living and the dead thinned so that spirits could enter our world. Kind of a cool time to be born, actually."

"Hey," I protest, "you're poaching! Samhain and ancient Celtic legend and folklore . . . that's all stuff we cover in AP English. That's my area." Okay, so I hadn't actually remembered Samhain and the Celtic folklore associated with Halloween until Gabe brought it up, but so what? He can't be smarter than I am about *everything*, can he? "You stick with physics and calculus and stuff like that."

He laughs. As he opens his book and pulls his assignment from it, he pushes aside my carton of french fries a little too quickly. The wind whisks away my half-done homework. "Aahh," I say, trying to leap up from the picnic table. My left foot gets stuck under Gabe's leg and I start to lose my balance. Laughing, Gabe grabs my arm to keep me from nose-diving into the table but makes the mistake of letting go of his own homework.

The wind seems to mock both of us as it picks up his paper and sends it fleeing in a different direction from mine. We each run off, laughing, in search of our homework.

is

I HAVE A STRANGE SENSE about that moment with Gabe at the picnic table. It's somehow essential. I don't know why it is, but it's the centerpiece of the puzzle of my existence. If I could just figure out what pieces are supposed to be attached to it, maybe I could . . .

Wait . . . I do know one of the reasons that moment is so essential.

Gabe is there.

I mean, the dead Gabe. I could feel his presence there just like I did when we lost our keys. It makes sense that he'd be there, too. After all, he also lost his homework when we were sitting at the picnic table.

I suppose it should be comforting to have him there—to have the company. But it's not.

Because Gabe's there, but I can't reach him.

I go in search of my physics homework. Is it still here? It should be. I remember now that we never found our homework. But one failing grade in physics . . . well, it just didn't seem that important after we'd gotten back together.

That's all I remember about that day, though. And it's . . . so near the end. I *do* know that.

Kristen was in labor that day, and I never found out whether the baby was a boy or girl. I'm sure of that. If I'd ever known who that baby was, it would have changed me somehow, become part of me. I mean, Kristen's my *sister.* There's a connection there that can't be broken, even by this death thing. I'm convinced I'd have the same connection to her child.

So *exactly* what did happen that day?

My physics homework is waiting for me, so I return . . . and return and return. . . .

But learn nothing.

Frustrated, I start flinging myself randomly back into all the moments of my life that I still have access to.

But nothing's changed in any of those moments. It's all still the same.

Until about my tenth time returning to the picnic table scene. . . .

the note

age 17

I'm so intent on my misery, I don't notice at first that I've been playing with my necklace . . . the one Gabe gave me last summer. It's silver, and at the center it has block letters that say FOREVER.

Yeah . . . so much for that. We aren't even talking now.

Tears blur my eyes, and I look down to see the words *I need to talk to you* written in strange handwriting. Definitely not mine.

How did that get on this piece of paper?

I'm startled by a soft touch on my shoulder, and I whirl around, gasping.

Gabe . . .

THE SONG OF MY LIFE has changed again. Even though I can't now remember what happened on my earlier trips to that picnic table, I can tell that a significant shake-up has happened. Something is fundamentally different in my world because . . . because Gabe left me a note on that piece of paper, and it wasn't the living Gabe who did it. It can't be. A ghost has been messing with that moment, and it doesn't feel like it was me. The other ghost in that moment was Gabe.

And he wants to talk to me.

I'm thrilled and full of longing but frustrated, too. I can't figure out how Gabe managed to leave me a note. My ghost can't go around leaving notes for other people. The only change I've ever managed to make to my life in a revisit is finding an object.

For a moment, I'm envious. Why does Gabe get to be a more advanced spirit than I am?

Maybe it's because he was better at physics than I was. Maybe it takes some kind of understanding that I don't have of quantum mechanics . . . all that simultaneous-communication-and-observation-of-sub-atomic-particles-changing-reality stuff.

Maybe. But probably not. He always did figure out life faster than I did (well, except when it came to his dad and the whole drinking thing). I shouldn't be surprised that he managed to figure out death faster, too.

So what's he doing differently than I am? I try to recall how my journeys back to life began. They started with the sweatshirt. Then there was the bracelet . . . which I found. Can't go back there to find the answer.

At least not the way I'm used to going back to moments.

But I can *remember* that moment. I have a nagging feeling that something was different about that visit than about the many others I've made since then. What was it?

Then it comes to me.

Ohmygod. It's been so obvious the whole time.

And I've missed it.

I don't have to *be* me when I'm experiencing those

moments. I can stay separate from myself . . . like I did the first few times I returned to my life. On my original visit to the sweatshirt moment, I stayed back and watched for a few minutes. I did the same thing when I used the bracelet. It was only when I pushed myself too close to, well, myself, that I was drawn back into the experience. Drawn like a magnet to a lodestone. I could have kept my distance. But I liked living too much. So every time I returned to a moment of my life, I *lived* it again instead of observing it.

For the first time ever in *Is*, I laugh. At least, I think that's what I'm doing. It's like every subatomic particle in my being is dancing with delight.

My mother was right. About everything.

The whole object attachment thing?

Right. Even in death, I've still been attached to those objects.

The whole you-have-trouble-with-change speech she gave me when I started middle school?

Right again. I haven't been able to let go of life.

My mother knows me so well that she even knows who I am when I'm dead.

It's time to experiment with observing instead of living. Who knows what will happen?

I know just the right experience to start with.

| unrattled |

KEEP BACK . . . KEEP BACK, I remind myself. If I want to watch this all happening, I have to keep my distance from that baby in the bouncy seat on the kitchen floor. It's difficult to do. There is a natural pull drawing me closer. I have to work hard to resist it, but, surprisingly, the longer I do, the easier it gets.

The force dragging me tapers off enough for me to notice what's actually going on. I'm cooing at my mom, who is across the room standing at the sink. She's not paying enough attention to me, so I coo louder. She notices the sounds, turns, and comes to get the baby me. As I get a good look at her, my first thought is, *Ohmygod . . . it's*

Mom, and she looks so *young.*

My second thought is, *Lose the outfit, Mom. Totally eight-ies and it's well into the nineties. And the hair? Definitely has to go. It's long and curly and, well,* bushy.

Being here but not being me (at least the original me) is way weird. This is a Mom that I've seen in pictures but don't actually remember. She's leaning toward the baby me, who (by the way) stinks. I've never been able to stand the smell of baby. Eau de spit-up, baby powder, and plastic dia-per? Yeah, no, thanks.

Smell, I notice, is a lot different for me in this hover-ing spiritual state. It's not as real as when I'm living the moment. I can still smell things, but it's like all those scents are coming from a great distance, as if they have to cross some kind of invisible boundary to get to me. That's the way sounds seem to work, too.

Mom doesn't care that the baby me smells so bad. She's talking baby talk, telling me what a cute baby I am and rubbing noses. It's a habit she didn't get rid of until I was older, so I have a clear memory of doing a lot of nose rub-bing with her.

I wonder if my spirit has any power over things in this moment. Can I, for instance, knock over that plate balanc-ing precariously on the edge of the counter? I sort of . . . will it to happen.

And it does.

Mom, startled, whirls around. "Whew . . ." she says as she realizes there's no immediate danger. She goes to the closet to get a broom. She cleans up the mess (I can't help feeling proud of myself for creating it) and then goes back and picks me up, snuggling and cuddling me. "Nothing to be scared of," she reassures me. "It was just a breeze knocking over the plate."

Ha. Just a breeze. As Mom puts baby me back in the bouncy seat, she chucks me under the chin, then moves toward the kitchen sink where she starts peeling carrots. I miss her already. Loneliness emanates from a tiny me and, like smell and sound, floats across the boundary between us, reaching me in the form of an echo.

Baby me starts cooing again. But when Mom doesn't respond, I begin playing with my rattle and knock it onto the floor. As it rolls under the cabinet, my crying brings Mom rushing over. She tries to hush me and then begins humming a lullaby. When neither of those work, she says, in a singsong voice, "What's the matter with my baby? Is she wet?"

Oh, get real, I want to tell her. I just lost my rattle. How hard is it to notice that?

Apparently, pretty hard. She picks me up, checks my diaper, realizes it isn't messy, and then starts trying to nurse me . . . *nurse me?! Ohmygod . . . this is so sick. I have to get out of here. Now!*

But how? I have to wait until my body moves a certain distance from the lost object, don't I?

Thank God the baby me isn't having anything to do with the whole nursing thing. I keep pulling away, and finally Mom decides to take me for a little walk down the hallway.

Released. Sent back to *Is*.

Thank God. Or the Universe. Or Whatever.

For the release, but also for graduating me to a new level in the spirit world. The Universe has actually given me more power than I thought it had. I can create changes in my original life from a ghost state, too.

Except . . .

Maybe this zipping around in and out of life as a spirit isn't such a cool idea after all. There are some things that we are not meant to know, understand, or see. Like my mom trying to nurse me, for example.

Besides, interfering in that moment has changed my original life again. I'm starting to feel that strange shifting of self. "It was just a silly plate I broke!" I find myself wanting to shout at the Universe.

Not that it would care, anyway.

The Universe just doesn't make the best of companions. I long for something more than it's giving me. I recall the note that Gabriel left at the picnic table: *I need to talk to you*.

Realization tingles through me: I've been too focused on *how* Gabe managed to leave me that note. Too focused on his desire to see me. I've been missing a possible implication of his words: Maybe we *can* talk.

I try to imagine how this would be possible. If I return to a moment that another ghost shares with me, and stay in the state I used for observation, will I encounter that other ghost?

I only know of two possible moments I share with another ghost and that I still have access to—the picnic table scene, and the Ouija board one. I consider both.

What if I'm wrong? What if I can't communicate with a ghost?

Better to have that happen when I'm expecting to encounter Tammy than Gabe. If it doesn't work, I'll be less disappointed.

Where's that hair clip?

| gathering as a ghost |

RETURNING TO THE NIGHT of the Ouija board is completely different from my last spiritual expedition. For one thing, we're in a basement. The humidity makes the air heavier, and it's harder for me to move around with this not-exactly-corporeal body.

But the big difference? That would be sharing space with another ghost. I mean, a real ghost. Tammy's ghost.

I'm watching things from a distance when she startles me by more or less saying, "Thought you were never gonna show up. I was starting to wonder if you were avoiding me."

I say "more or less" because it turns out that ghosts don't actually *talk* to each other in the same sense that living humans do. I'm not sure what you'd call it. Certainly it's some form of communication. And clear enough communication that I know what she's telling me. It's just that there aren't any, well, words. There're just . . . *ideas*. I'm not sure how to respond to her, because how can you talk to someone when you aren't really talking?

Turns out I don't have to worry about it. I'm confused by her "Thought you were never gonna show up" statement (since I've been here what seems like a million times) and think, *What's she talking about?* She immediately tells me, "You. Coming here. As a spirit. So I could actually have a conversation with you."

It's like . . . whatchamacallit—telepathic communication.

We're communicating telepathically, and whoa . . . not such a good thing. I mean, what if somehow she reads my mind and I'm thinking something that I don't really want her to know?

"Oh, in time you'll learn how to keep some ideas back from other spirits. It's just that you have to learn all over again how to communicate . . . both the truth and lies."

Great. Like learning to communicate the first time wasn't hard enough?

"Doesn't take all that long. You'll catch on quickly. This must be your first attempt at communicating with another spirit."

"Well, yeah. It's not like I've experienced many moments where I lost something at the same time some other dead person I know did. In fact, I've only discovered two other moments like that, and one of them I can't get to anymore. I found the stupid keys that would take me there."

"Oh. Don't worry," Tammy reassures me. "You'll find more moments like that. You have eternity to do it."

Not exactly reassuring.

"And the more experience you get hanging out with other spirits, the better you'll communicate with us."

"Well, my only practice so far has been when I was thirteen and talking to you through the Ouija board."

"Oh, yeah, sorry about that."

"That reminds me. The whole thing where you used the Ouija board to apologize? Do you think you could be a little clearer about that? I mean, what are you sorry for?"

Neither of us has a body. I know this misty whiteness next to me is Tammy because . . . well, I just do. The same way I know what she's saying to me. When I ask her that question, it's like all her whiteness becomes brighter, and I know this is a form of laughter. I don't find anything here particularly funny.

"Did you kill me? Is that why you're sorry?"

The glow of laughter disappears. She darkens with what seems like . . . regret. Just when I'm thinking I have the answer to my question, she surprises me.

"Of course I have regrets. But they aren't about *killing* you. I mean, how could you even think it? I would *never* kill someone who had once been my friend."

I don't know if I'm more stunned by the loyalty she's expressing or the way she's kind of left open the possibility that she might kill someone who wasn't once her friend.

She interrupts my thoughts: "*Don't* even go there. Of course I wouldn't kill anyone. I might have made my mistakes, but murder was never one of them."

"Then what *are* you sorry for?"

"Thinking you ratted me out. I found out later who did it, but before that I thought it was you. And I should have realized you'd never do that to me."

"You're right. You had enough trouble in your life without me adding to it. Not that I ever knew *what* exactly that trouble was."

"And you never will."

I can deal with that. I mean, not that I have much choice . . . not having all these mind-reading skills yet that Tammy has. Still, I have to admit that being dead has given me something of an appreciation for mystery. I kind of like that there are things I *don't* understand.

Well . . . except for the whole how-I-died thing.

"Wait, you mean you don't know how you died?" Tammy asks me. She glows again. Surprise this time.

"You mean you *do* know how *you* died?"

"Of course. I remember it well. Had a car accident."

"How old were you?"

"Thirty-five."

Whoa . . . she lived to be thirty-five? Something here doesn't seem fair. The drug dealer lives to thirty-five, and the good girl dies at seventeen? "Hold on. . . . That means you . . . you know things that I don't, things that happened after I died."

"Well, yeah. Of course. What do you want to know?"

Starting with something safe seems like a good idea. "Did Amber and Lacey actually go to prom with Doug Preston and Scott Turner?"

"Why would I know *that*? I'm not omniscient. I only know what I noticed when I was alive. I couldn't have cared less who they went to prom with senior year. Didn't pay any attention."

"But you said . . . I mean, the Ouija board said that they went to prom with those two."

Bright white laughter. "Yeah. I was just playing a trick on them."

"A trick?!"

"You have to admit their reactions were kind of funny. Gotta entertain myself somehow. But senior prom isn't really what you want to know about, is it?"

"No," I admit. Here goes . . . "Do you know how *I* died?"

Inside the mist, some kind of strange whirling takes place. Indecision.

"This isn't a tough question. I mean, you either know or you don't."

"I know."

This is the moment when she's supposed to tell me the answer I've been searching for . . . isn't it? I wait patiently, but she doesn't reveal anything.

"Well? Tell me!"

"I don't think so. Seems like if you were ready to know, you'd know."

"Oh, I'm ready. Trust me."

"There are some things you have to find out for yourself. Other people can't tell them to you."

Wonderful. Now she sounds like one of our parents or something. How did that happen?

"I became one."

"Became what?" I ask.

"A parent."

Okay, this whole mind-reading business is irritating. "Get out of here. You? A parent?"

"Four kids. Three boys and a girl. The youngest was less than a year when I died."

In life, this is one of those moments where you have to fall into the nearest chair because you're so shocked. As a spirit, you just do this weird kind of separating thing. This is truly the first time I've understood what it meant that life went on without me. Even though I *knew* it would, a part of me didn't accept that. I was the center of all the stories I knew. It was even kind of hard to believe, in a way, that anyone existed when they weren't with me . . . even though I knew they did. But this . . . this whole life I don't even know about? How much of the world changed without me knowing it?

I realize that Tammy hasn't interrupted any of my thoughts. This is the longest she's let me have a conversation with myself since I arrived here. Very parentlike, very let-the-kid-make-her-own-discovery and all that. She isn't the girl I knew in my life.

"Not true," she argues. "I might be radically different, but I'm still me."

I remember Tammy's first comment . . . that she thought I was avoiding her and would never get here. "Have you been waiting here for me all this time?"

"Kind of."

"I don't get it. How can you 'kind of' wait for me?"

"It's like this: if you don't attach yourself when you come back to visit your life, if you stand back here and watch, then you exist in a separate time frame from the life events. It's the same time frame that exists in the space where your lost objects are."

Right. Makes perfect sense. Almost. "Then how are you

only 'kind of' here? Don't you either wait or *not* wait?"

"No . . . not really. Eventually you'll learn you can be in more than one place when you're a spirit. Part of me can hang out here waiting for you, but other parts of me can go somewhere else for a while. I've just been keeping part of me here while also wandering off to do other things, too."

"Are you . . . *all* here now?"

"Yep."

A blanket of longing for the Tammy I knew in life encompasses me. I can't help being touched that our friendship meant so much to her that she's been trying this hard to reach me. "Why did you . . . why have you been waiting so long for me?"

"I wanted to make sure we cleared the air about things. I feel terrible about blaming you for my getting caught selling drugs. After you died, I still thought for a few weeks that it was you who ratted on me. I hated you. Wouldn't even go to your funeral. Was glad you were dead, in fact. Until I found out the truth. I felt incredibly guilty after that. Especially for hating you even after you were dead. That's what I was trying to apologize for. Well, that and the way our friendship ended on the night of the slumber party."

"I was always sorry about that, too. But . . . what happened originally at the slumber party that broke up our friendship? I mean, before you came back to this moment as a ghost and tried to apologize."

"I guess neither of us is ever going to know much about that, are we? I remember that before I messed with things, we *were* playing with a Ouija board. And something *did* happen with it that caused us to have a fight. But now the only reality we can remember is the one where I apologize to you through the Ouija board. Unless, of course, we want a new reality and decide to go back and change this whole experience again."

"Probably not a good idea," I say.

"Agreed."

I can't help having second thoughts. "Even though it might save our friendship if we did . . . ?"

"It also might not, Maddy. I think the end of our living friendship was all part of the experience we were meant to have."

"*Meant* to have?" I ask. "Is there a God somewhere orchestrating our lives? Because if there is, I haven't met Him . . . Her . . . yet."

"God . . . well, I guess you could call it that if you want. There's something beautiful and powerful beyond us, and that's enough for me. But it doesn't really orchestrate our lives. We're just meant to be us. So we are. And we're meant to make the best choices we can. So I do. Apologizing to you through the Ouija board was one of those choices. What took you so long to finally decide to communicate with me here in this moment?"

"I didn't know how," I admitted.

"What do you mean?"

I confess, "I've kind of only had one other experience where I just watched what was happening when I went back to my life. All the other times I've used a lost item, I've always *become* me in the experience."

"Wow. You've really had a major case of separation anxiety, haven't you? Really wanted to keep living?"

"Didn't you?"

"Not so much. What I wanted was to know how my kids and husband were. How they changed over the years. What became of them. And when I realized I couldn't, I just stopped caring about living. I almost never do it anymore. Life gets boring after a while, you know?"

Unfortunately, I do. Reliving something over and over just isn't the same thing as . . . well, *living* it.

Tammy continues, "I prefer to leave life alone and spend time in the Everafter."

"What's that?"

The glowing flares up again. "What's attaching you so strongly to life?"

"How am I supposed to know?" Even as I ask it, I know it's a stupid question. *I'm* the only one who *would* know. "Can you get back here from the Everafter anytime you want?"

"Of course. Once you get to the Everafter, though, you

won't care so much about being here."

"What's it like there?"

"You'll just be a part of everything. All at once. You'll finally feel as if you belong somewhere . . . at least, I did. You'll like it. Once you get there. Just go there."

"How?"

"Find out how you died. Maybe that's what's keeping you here."

"I'm trying. Can you at least give me a hint?"

"Find Gabe. I think he has the answers you want. I don't know if he'll give them to you, but he might help you find them."

Gabe.

Of course.

"How do I get out of here?" I ask. "Do I have to wait until my real body gets too far away from that hair clip I lost? I mean, that's how I've always done it before . . . either that or I've found the object."

I can tell that if she had a head, Tammy would be shaking it at me in despair. "Stop thinking so much. Just be. That's enough. Let yourself be what you want, when you want, where you want. Just decide you want to do something, and you'll end up doing it."

Sounds easy. Yeah, right. . . .

Except it is. It works the first time I try it.

am

I AM . . . I AM . . . I AM . . . floating. This isn't *Is*. It's *Am*. I'm not located here, the way I first thought I was.

I *am* here. And I'm not trapped here.

For the first time, I realize how beautiful this space is, how it brims with vital energy.

I'm relieved to discover that my conversation with Tammy hasn't changed anything about our original moments of life in that basement. Standing outside an event and watching it—as long as I don't try to change anything by knocking over silly plates and stuff like that—seems to have no effect on my original life.

I don't have to be alone anymore. I can communicate

with other spirits when I meet them in moments where we both lost objects. And I don't have to sacrifice who I am—and what I was—in order to do it.

Tammy's right. I need to find Gabe. It's time.

I start looking for my physics homework.

THE FIRST THING I REALIZE about the misty Gabe is that I miss being able to reach out and touch him. And, I know this sounds superficial, but I miss the way he looks. I mean, he was *hot* and now he's just mist. I know . . . I know . . . this is the kind of thing that keeps me attached to life and makes me a decidedly unenlightened spirit.

But it's true. And I have to admit it.

The second thing I realize about him is that he's glowing with happiness to see me.

The third thing I realize—with a tremendous amount of relief—is that he isn't reading my mind in the same way Tammy did. Either he doesn't have the ability that she does, or . . . maybe he respects my privacy more.

"I still love you," he says right away. I'm glad that came before anything else he might communicate to me.

"And I still love you," I tell him. "How long have you been waiting for me to figure out how to reach you?"

"I don't know. It doesn't matter, does it?"

Maybe. I mean, a girl doesn't want her boyfriend to be better at *every*thing than she is, does she? "I don't know," I tell him.

"It doesn't matter to me. I'd wait as long as I needed to for you."

"Have you been to the Everafter? This place that Tammy tells me is so great?"

"No. I've heard about it, though."

"From who?"

"My father. I met him in one of the moments of my life. Like I am with you now."

"Oh . . . I'm sorry. About your dad dying, I mean. . . ."

There's a smile in Gabe's glow. "Maddy, there's nothing to be sorry about. I can see him whenever I want. I lost a Star Wars action figure, a Luke Skywalker, when I was seven. Dad lost some change at the same time."

"You are lucky, then. I mean . . . I haven't run into my family anywhere. I'd like to be able to talk to them in . . . this form. But so far I haven't encountered an object that takes me to a moment when any of them also lost something."

"Oh, I think you'll run into them somewhere."

"I hope so. You know what the weirdest feeling about that is?"

"What?"

"Knowing somewhere in all this crazy time they're already dead. Even when they're alive, they're dead, right? I mean, that's the way it is with us. We're dead but visiting this moment where we're also alive, so we're both alive and dead in the same moment. The same thing is happening to all the people we knew and loved. Time's all wrinkled up on itself, like a Kleenex that's been all smushed together. It touches itself in all these different places."

As reassuring as this is, I hope that my family isn't stuck somewhere on the edge of the Kleenex, in a place that doesn't fold back onto any of the creases I'm occupying.

"You'll see your family again, Maddy. I'm sure of it."

He's a mind reader, too? What am I, the joke of the Universe? The only ghost in the Great Expanse who doesn't know *anything* about navigating the spiritual experience? "You can read minds, too. Just like Tammy." It's an accusation. I can't help it. I feel a little betrayed.

"Huh?"

I explain to him what happened when I visited Tammy at the slumber party. He seems surprised. "Well, I suppose it makes as much sense as everything else I've discovered since I died," he admits. "But I haven't learned to do that yet. I wasn't reading your mind. I was reading *you*."

"What do you mean?"

"Maddy, how much time did we spend together? I *know* you. You're always worried about whether the people you love will be there for you when you need them. You're always afraid something will tear them away from you."

"Well, I was right, wasn't I? I mean, *here* I am, and my family's *not* here, are they?"

"I'm here."

That's *so* Gabe. Just two simple words, but they mean everything to me.

"Besides, who knows exactly what we'll find in the Everafter? Dad says that when you're there, you're with everyone you ever loved, that they become space and you fall into them. You'll become them, and they'll become you. *Every-one* is there, according to him, even if they're not dead yet, because they're, well, already dead somewhere."

Who knew Gabe's dad could be so poetic? I bet he's lounging around in the Everafter with Emily Dickinson and my mother. They're having great debates about the meaning of death and loss.

While *becoming* one another, of course.

Not that I'm bitter or anything. "So if the Everafter's that great, why haven't you gone there yet? Can't you get there?"

"I don't know. I think I could. But I don't want to go yet.

I'm waiting for you. And you aren't ready."

"Tammy thinks it's because I don't know how I died. She thinks that's keeping me tied here. She also thinks you can help me figure out what happened to me. *Do* you know how I died?"

"Yes."

"How come you know and I don't?" I demand. I might be sounding a little like, well, a spoiled five-year-old.

"Your back was turned. Mine wasn't."

I'm so surprised by this statement that my mist seems to scatter in several directions. I'm in danger of dispersing into an Expanding Universe. Gabe's mist surrounds me and keeps me centered enough to fold back in on myself.

"You *saw* it happen?"

"Yes. And I wish I hadn't."

"Why don't you tell me about it, then?" I ask. "Afterward, we can float off together into the sunset, or the clouds, or whatever we float off into to get to the Everafter."

We swirl without communicating for a moment. Finally, Gabe says, "I think you'll need to see it for yourself. Even if I wish I hadn't seen it, I think you need to."

"Have you ever been back to that real moment?"

"Yeah. A few times. I never want to go again."

"How'd you get there?"

"The necklace. The one you're playing with over there. The one I gave you as a present."

I look over to where the living Gabe and I are sitting at a picnic table talking.

Oh, yeah. Guess I kind of forgot about them. I mean, us.

I was busy paying attention to the other us.

Gabe continues, "I think it's been with me in *Everywhere* this whole time."

"*Everywhere?* What's that?" I ask, but then I suddenly know what he's talking about. "Oh. *Everywhere.* That must be what I call *Is.*"

"Yeah, *Everywhere* is kind of an . . . *Is.*"

"Yeah, except lately I've started thinking of it as *Am*, because, you know, while I'm there, I just kind of am . . . well, *everywhere*, I guess." My brain is starting to get tangled. "So why would my necklace have been in *Everywhere* with you?" I ask.

"I happened to be holding it just before . . . I mean, I dropped it a second before we died. I guess that counts as me losing it."

We. We died. He died with me? I suspected as much, but hearing it is still distressing.

"So how am I supposed to get back to that final moment of our lives? I need to have lost an object in that final moment in order to get back to it."

"You did lose something. It's just not exactly an object."

"What are you talking about?"

"Your life. You lost it there. That gives you free entry, my dad says. I've never tried to do it. I have the necklace with me in *Everywhere*, so I've never needed to find my lost life there."

?!?!

Have I wasted all this time revisiting my life when all along I had access to finding out how I died? Just by finding my "life" in *Is*?

"And how—exactly—am I supposed to find my life in *Is*?" I ask. "I have no idea what it even looks like. Is this some kind of Peter Pan thing? You know . . . find your shadowy life and sew it back on so it can't get away again?"

Gabe's presence is smiling all around me. "Maybe it is. Who knows? But I'm sure you'll figure it all out. Maybe it has something to do with that whole 'am' thing you were talking about. Try thinking something, you know, like 'I am my life.'"

"It's worth a try. Will you come back to the moment of our death with me?" Facing this alone is terrifying. Besides, now that I've found Gabe again, I don't want to be without him for a single second. Even as I'm asking the question, though, I can tell from the feeling emanating off of him that he's going to say no.

"My ghost will just be a distraction to you while you're trying to see what's happening. Besides, I've already been there, and I don't think I can bear to watch it all again.

Remember you won't be totally without me. The living me will still be there."

"And after I've seen what happened? Will you meet me back here?"

"Of course."

I realize I might just as well get on with this whole thing so I can come back and see Gabe again.

And then move on with him to the Everafter.

"I love you," I tell Gabe.

"I love you, too," he says.

And then I return myself to *Am*.

```
┌─────────┐
│         │
│   am    │
│         │
└─────────┘
```

AM ROCKS ME BACK AND FORTH like a baby. I feel my soul-beat pounding against the bubble of space I inhabit here. I concentrate on the feeling of it, the comfort of knowing that the energy that is me still stretches its wings, longs to expand.

I am my life, I think, and instantly something indefinable emerges within all the energy that is me. It's not at all like Peter Pan's shadow, which struggled for its freedom. That something is happy to be a part of me. It dances and jumps, filling me with a giddy tingling. We float through the *Am* of *Is* on the way to find . . .

the end

GABE AND I ARE STEPPING out of his father's car. We're at Sandra's house. It's odd watching action I'd rather be feeling. I know—but only from a strange distance—what the pavement of the driveway must feel like under my feet. The temptation to become me is greater when there's no spirit Gabe or spirit Tammy to distract me.

"This clasp is broken," the living me says to Gabe. I'm looking down at the FOREVER necklace he gave me, trying to bend the clasp ring farther open so I can refit the chain link onto the end of it. Of course I stumble over a rock in the driveway. I've never been good at walking and trying to do something else at the same time.

Gabe reaches out and steadies me. I look up at him and kiss him. "Would you see if you can fix this? I don't want to lose it," I say, handing the necklace to him.

Now that I'm here, I remember all this. But how did a simple trip to Sandra's house after school wind up being the final scene of my life? It doesn't make sense. I start trying to run through everything I remember about living the experience, only to discover that I'm missing important things as they're playing out in front of me.

So much for trying to remember. Gabe and I are already halfway into the house. I have to go all Casper and swish my way through the door while it's still open.

"What's wrong?" I'm asking Sandra. Dressed in old jeans and a ratty sweatshirt, she's standing in front of us, blocking the hallway to keep us from going any farther into the house. There's a strange silence invading everything. A scary one.

But the look on Sandra's face is even scarier. I've never seen anything like it before. The living me knows that it's a frightening expression, but the misty me recognizes its depth of desperation in a way I never could have when I was living. There's something dying behind those green eyes.

"What's wrong?" I ask Sandra.

Gabe is alarmed enough at her expression that he's put his arm around her shoulders and is trying to lead her to the living room. "Go get Sandra a glass of water, why don't you?" he says to me.

I move toward the kitchen, but Sandra starts crying. "No," she says. "You've got to leave, Maddy. My mom is completely losing it."

"Where's your dad?" I ask.

"I don't know. I've been trying to reach him for a few hours now. He left for work this morning, but he's not there now, and his cell is turned off. I've just never seen my mom quite like this before."

Gabe has managed to push her gently into the living room and has settled her onto the couch.

"Where's your mom right now?" I ask.

"Upstairs. Look, you guys, you need to go."

"Is she threatening to kill herself again, Sandra? Maybe you should call the police if she is. I mean, we can't really handle that, you know?"

"Just go, please."

"You have to come with me, Sandra. I can't leave you here."

"I can't go with you."

"Yes, you can. And you know what? Today I came up with a brilliant solution to your problem. You can come live with us for the rest of the school year. I know my parents will let you. My mom thinks you're great. And she knows how crazy your mom is. She won't want you to stay here. And she'll understand how important it is not to have to leave school your senior year. It's a great solution. Gets you away from your mom but lets you stay close enough to check on her."

"Maddy, whatever. I'll talk to you about it later, okay? Just go right now." She stands up and leads us back toward the front door.

Sandra keeps glancing over her shoulder, but the living me doesn't pay any attention to where Sandra's looking. I'm so busy trying to convince her to leave with me that I don't notice Mrs. Simpson coming down the stairs.

But the misty me sees her, sees the horrible expression on Mrs. Simpson's face. She's never liked me, and the look on her face now tells me she's moved beyond dislike. The current of her hatred is an undertow, ready to pull all of us into the depths of a furious ocean.

Mrs. Simpson keeps moving down the stairs. Both her hands are behind her back. She follows us toward the door with frighteningly soft and purposeful steps. Her lips are moving, but I can't hear what she's saying because the living me is pleading so loudly with Sandra.

I mist myself closer to Mrs. Simpson and hear her mumbling, "You won't take her away from me. You won't take her away from me. That's what you've always wanted. But I won't let you do it."

She's pulling one of her arms from behind her back. She has a gun in her hand. A ray of sunlight coming from the open front door catches the flat black side of the metal barrel. The reflected beam of light gleams with an incongruent beauty. Mrs. Simpson raises her arm, pointing the gun at my back as I stand with Sandra by the door.

The gun's trigger is gold. It stands out against the deathly black of the rest of the gun. I've never before felt threatened by anything gold-colored, and yet I understand what is about to happen. My life will end.

Mrs. Simpson brings her second arm around to the front, using a two-handed grip on the gun. I want to shout at myself, tell myself to run, save my life. I don't have time to think about whether I should change the past. I have to do it. I have to save myself and Gabe.

Only it's not that simple.

Gabe has turned and sees Mrs. Simpson. He's wearing an expression of utter shock, whispering, "Jesus Christ." I can tell what he's about to do, and I have to stop him. I can't seem to save us both. I don't have time to think . . . it's all happening so fast.

Gabe drops the necklace and lunges at Mrs. Simpson. She sees him coming and swings her arms around to point the gun at him. The only thing I have time to do is use all my energy to push back against the gun, to move its muzzle so it isn't pointing at Gabe anymore. The gun is in wild movement as a shot is fired. The shot whizzes toward me, where I'm standing next to Sandra at the door. Alive.

For only a fraction of a second longer.

Everything goes blank. Dead. Even the spirit me is not allowed to see what happens next.

Thank God.

I wouldn't be able to bear seeing the expression on Sandra's face as she realizes her mother has killed me.

after the end

I'M BACK IN *AM*, surrounded by all the objects that have taken me on so many journeys.

Strange . . .

They don't attract me at all anymore. I don't want to go back and see any of those scenes of my life.

They all end the same way.

If I changed any of the individual scenes, eventually, it would all end the same, wouldn't it? I could go back to the final scene and try again to save Gabe and myself, but I'd only be prolonging my life. I might find out what happens with Kristen and the baby. Or who my friends go to prom with. I might even marry and have children of my own.

But eventually I'd have to die, wouldn't I?

And no matter when I left, I'd always wonder about someone. Would it be any better to be in Tammy's situation? I mean, wondering whatever happened to your own children?

I don't think I'm any better off knowing how I died than I was when I didn't know. Finding out is kind of deflating, actually. It seems like I haven't accomplished anything by solving this mystery.

Except . . . I realize that's not quite true. Because what I've accomplished is understanding that mystery can be a *good* thing. There are some things it's good not to know, because when you don't, the Universe is full of possibilities. I guess I now realize, too, that . . . well, it's okay to die. I didn't *want* to die. I'm glad it's not my fault that I did, but what's happened has already happened. There truly *is* a time to live and a time to die. Maybe all that is what I actually needed to know—not *how* I died.

Besides, knowing how I died has brought me pain and regret, too. I recognize how destroyed Sandra must feel about what happened, and I don't have any way to let her know I understand this is not her fault. I can't tell her that even though I'm dead, I'm fine. Not unless I want to leave her a note at the death scene, which would probably scare her half to death and make her think she's losing her sanity. She probably already thinks she is, anyway. No. A note would just be too cruel. I have to wait to stumble upon her out here in the Universe somewhere before I can have that conversation with her.

In the meantime, I have to trust that somehow she'll be fine. Like I am.

Now it's time to find Gabe.

Even though I never saw what happened after Mrs. Simpson shot me, I know Gabe died, too, even after I tried to change things. I can sense his spirit in the Universe with me. I locate my physics homework. . . . "Well?" he wants to know as soon as I arrive at the picnic table.

It feels good to be back with him, but for all my new-found love of mystery, there are still some questions I wouldn't mind having the answers to. "How did it happen," I ask him, "those final moments? I mean, in the original version? Because I tried to change how things turned out and now I wonder what originally happened. From the time Mrs. Simpson raised the gun, I mean."

"I don't exactly remember because I changed the moment, too. I wanted to prevent us both from dying. I remember that, and I remember going back to change things. Only it didn't work. We still ended up dead. And when I got back to *Everywhere*, I had already lost all my memories of the original events. I could only remember the new ones—that and the fact that I'd somehow changed things. And now all I can remember from that final scene is what happened when *you* changed it."

"I tried to save you but ended up killing me. Did she shoot you right after she killed me?"

"Yeah. I remember that for a split second she seemed surprised, and then she turned on me and shot me."

"Do you think we could ever change the outcome of that scene?" I ask him. "Maybe we can work together to do it somehow." I know, even while I'm saying it, that we shouldn't, but I need to hear that from Gabe.

"I don't know. No matter what we do, we might end up dead. The question is, do we want to risk trying again and again to save ourselves? We could end up killing Sandra, too."

This is a horrifying idea. I can't believe I didn't realize it back when I was trying to save Gabe. That wild shot hit me, but it was only inches away from hitting Sandra instead. I tell Gabe, "There's no way I'm going to risk that happening. I know that whatever time Sandra has left to live will be shadowed by what she saw her mother do to us, but I want her to live. I know she'll make the world a better place."

"You did, too," Gabe tells me.

I'm taken off guard by the compliment. It's the nicest thing anyone's ever said to me. "You, too," I say, meaning it. "But our chance at that has passed. I don't want to spend eternity trying to change what's already happened. I want to move on."

I'm ready.

Ready to allow what might have been to remain a mystery. Ready to check out the Everafter. Ready to find out if immortality will "unveil a third event to me," as Emily Dickinson said.

Maybe I can hang out with her in the Everafter . . . her and my mother and Gabe's father, all of us really understanding what life and death mean.

"I want to move on with you," Gabe tells me.

We float there for a moment uncertainly. "Do you know how to get to the Everafter?" Gabe finally asks.

"Do you?"

"No."

"Tammy said we'd be able to do it when the time was right. I think it's like everything else. We just let ourselves *be* there."

And suddenly that's what we're doing. Everything hums and buzzes with peaceful electricity. Warmth without heat, satisfaction without gain, being everything and nothing all at once . . . and losing language. I feel it slipping away from me, but I don't miss it as it floats off on a wave, my life and all its words closing for the second time.

James Madison Frazier

BORN: OCTOBER 31
1:35 AM

To Kristen and John Frazier

8 POUNDS, 11 OUNCES

I was always a Robert Frost kind of girl. My best friend, Madison, wasn't. Emily Dickinson was her favorite poet. I never understood why until Maddy died.

Much of Frost's poetry has a rhythm or rhyme that has always pleased and comforted me. When he begged me to think about "The Road Not Taken," I believed in the power to choose. When he observed, "Some say the world will end in fire, / Some say in ice" I never minded wondering which would be the case because he also reminded me that I have ". . . miles to go before I sleep."

Emily Dickinson, however, I used to consider downright weird. Her poems were too focused on death. Full of pain and even occasionally cynicism, they left me feeling hopeless.

My attitude about all that changed, though, when Madison died. When I turned to Robert Frost's poetry for comfort, I found none. His assertion that he had "miles to go before I sleep" frightened me. After all, I was facing miles of life without Madison. My world had ended in fire, and I was left wondering whether I could have prevented Madison's death if I'd traveled a different road on the day she died. And then, in the poem "Out, out—" Frost hit me with a callous truth. Of a dead boy's family and friends, he wrote, "And they, since they / Were not the one dead, turned to their affairs." All around me, so many people seemed to be treating Maddy's death that way. Dates were made for dances, and teachers went on assigning homework.

In the midst of my grief, it was Emily Dickinson who comforted me. When I read her poetry, it was almost as if she were in the room with me. Don't ask me whether I mean Madison or the poet. I'm not sure. Perhaps they both were.

There were moments when I was reading Dickinson when I was horrified. I wasn't sure if the "he" in the following poem meant Death or God:

He stuns you by degrees—
. . . Deals—One—imperial—Thunderbolt—
That scalps your naked Soul—

I wondered if Madison felt she'd been dealt an "imperial thunderbolt" as she lay dying on the entryway floor of my house. I certainly felt as if my naked soul had been scalped. The horror these lines made me feel kept me reading more of Dickinson's poetry, and I discovered Dickinson understood what I was feeling:

> *The last Night that She lived*
> *It was a Common Night*
> *Except the Dying—this to Us*
> *Made Nature different*
>
> *We noticed smallest things—*
> *Things overlooked before*
> *By this great light upon our Minds*
> *Italicized—as 'twere.*

Dickinson expressed so well the way that Maddy's death has italicized her life upon my heart: her smile, her support, our Halloween antics, and our late-night sleepovers. These small things, so overlooked before, are etched upon my heart, where Maddy will go on living for as long as I do.

acknowledgments

Thanks many times over to my husband and daughter for putting up with me during the writing, revising, and editing of this novel. I also want to thank my parents, sister, and brother-in-law. Your support through the last few years has been invaluable. I'm further grateful to my sister for the language expertise she contributed to this book.

April, Ann, Deb, Kay, Lori, Ruth, and Tim: You really are the World's Greatest Critique Group; I'd have been lost if you hadn't adopted me. Special thanks to Donna Dunlap for being the first reader of this manuscript and encouraging me to keep up with it. I'm grateful to John Olstad for looking over my physics sections. Any of the mathematical incompatibilities between Einstein's theory of relativity and the theories of quantum mechanics that still appear in this novel are due to my use of poetic license; he gave me fair warning.

I'm grateful to my agents, Josh and Tracey Adams, for believing in this novel. I'd also like to thank my editor, Donna Bray, for pushing me to make this a better book, and Ruta Rimas, her assistant, for helping to guide me through this process.